Shoal

Shoal

A scintillating sci-fi suitable for children aged 10 to 13

Copyright © 2024 by Ian Hornett
All rights reserved. No part of this publication may be reproduced distributed or transmitted in any form or by any means including photocopying recording or other electronic or mechanical methods without the prior written permission of the author.
ISBN: 9798877044609

For

The children I have taught.

Marcus

When I was a very young kid, I used to lie awake in my bed for hours staring at the Spiderman wallpaper, trying to spot a detail in one of his many cool poses I hadn't spotted before. I was trying to put off the time when I had to go to sleep. Even then, I think I knew that trouble lay ahead.

When I eventually closed my eyes, I would see coloured dots streaming in from the left and right, swooping and sweeping across my private world – tiny specks of life, like a shoal of fish, moving as one in complete harmony.

Sometimes, they'd change direction, flowing backwards then forwards, or suddenly dart up and down, before speeding across from corner to corner.

I thought I was special. I never told anyone about my shoals of fish, not even Mum or Dad. It was my secret. My beautiful secret.

A beautiful secret, until the dots weren't beautiful anymore. Gradually, their movements became more frantic and jerkier. They seemed scared, as if they were desperate to get away from something, much like a real shoal of fish might when being hunted by sharks. Sleep for me wasn't sleep anymore. It became a nightmare battle as the dots crashed around in front of me. Terrifying hours of tossing and turning in the night. I'd go downstairs and talk rubbish to my parents, trying desperately to describe what was happening. I made no sense to them because it made no sense to me.

It all seemed very real, but I struggled to explain what was happening and how it made me feel.

It was not unusual, my parents were told. These were bad dreams that, someday, I would grow out of. But they were worried. I could tell they were.

One day, when I was older, I shared my secret world. Not with another person, but with a science book. I love science, all types but especially biology. I want to learn everything I can about the human body, be a doctor or, even better, a famous scientist who invents something to help the world.

I looked up in my book what it said about seeing dots when you close your eyes:

Phosphenes – electrical charges, caused by direct stimulation, other than by light.

You can get them when you sneeze or stand up too quickly. *"Gently touch your eyeballs with your eyes closed,"* the book said, *"and coloured dots will appear."* Prisoners, too long in a dark cell, experience them. Isaac Newton, the Greeks, scientists from way back – everyone knew about them. A lot of people see them.

But people don't see them, not my ones, anyway. Mine are different. Mine are mine. Yours are yours. His, hers, theirs; none of them are the same as mine.

And it would be better for you – all of you – if it stayed that way, believe me.

Because my private display of shoaling fish is telling me something.

They tell me your future, our future, the future of mankind. The future of everything.

I have to tell you: it's not looking good.

It's not looking good at all...

Part 1 – To the Beginning

Milo 8

Her name is Rose-Anne. She's just over a year older than me – fourteen – blonde, quite tall, has blue eyes, is funny, clever, good fun to be with, went to a real school, rather than just learning through downloads like the rest of us. (Going to a real school with proper people, a classroom and pens and stuff is a nice touch, these days). She loves playing sports and, like me, enjoys virtual surfing at weekends.

She is the perfect girlfriend in every way. Well, I say 'girlfriend'... she's a girl and a friend, so, in my book, that kinda counts as being a girlfriend.

She wants to meet me at the coffee bar. Her choice, not mine. I hate coffee. Bit young for it, I think. But I tell her 'Yes' because I can't refuse anything she asks. And it's good to have healthy disagreements, otherwise life up here on the disc would be so boring. (She's determined to get me using the natural coffee bean like they used to grow from plants on Earth, rather than the synthetic bean they make in labs. Won't work. To me, anything that starts life in a pile of dirt just doesn't seem right).

I see her now sitting on the stool, playing with the braids in her hair. She's wearing the silver top I helped her choose. Of course, it suits her; everything she wears suits her. Her hair is up, enough of the fringe hanging loose so that she can brush it away now and then. I love that. She does it in a modest way, not a "look at me, I'm so beautiful" way. I love her eyebrows, too: natural, no work on them at all, beautifully rounded at the ends. Her left one goes up slightly above the other when she says something funny or teases me. She's just...well... perfect!

Rose-Anne smiles broadly as she sees me, and I catch a glimpse of her (perfect) white teeth.

"I'm fifteen minutes from port," I tell her. "Landing might take longer than usual, but I should be with you in half an hour. Need to nip back to my living box first."

"No problem, Milo 8," she answers. "I can wait. The coffee is delicious. You'll adore it!" That eyebrow arches up. "I'm happy."

She is always happy. I want to stay longer talking to her, but I have to concentrate on other things. Landing the space freighter I pilot is only ninety percent automatic. All the information about the stellar winds is fed to the processor in my brain, but the final adjustments and decisions are human-led. The universe can be a bit dodgy and it needs human judgement to make sure all goes well.

Shoal

I wave goodbye, and then I'm gone from the cosy surroundings of the coffee bar. The reality of the cabin forms around me once more, and I get down to the serious business of landing the ship safely.

I'm logged by base as 'docking', one of only two of my daily activities (the other is take-off) that cannot be overridden by a compulsoral.

What's a compulsoral? Well, it's thirty minutes a day of compulsory commercials (shortened to compulsoral) that everyone has to do. They love selling us stuff here. Since Earth was abandoned a hundred years ago, the government has to find a way to make things work. That takes money. The thousand or so discs humans live on now that orbit the Earth and moon are like islands, kinda cities in space. We trade with each other to support the people that live on them. Our one – Disc 14.2 (such a great name… not!) – trades in rocks and metals from other planets, which is why I'm a freighter pilot who spends his days pulling huge lumps of the stuff around space.

I admit, I'm young to be a pilot. I was identified at the age of ten as being some sort of whizz-kid. I loved (still do!) playing *Space Adventure*; basically, a game where you pretend to be a pilot who has to deal with challenging situations on alien planets. I got ranked as a *Gold Star Pilot*, the highest possible ranking. Someone important in the Space Academy linked into one of my games one day, saw I was good at it, and recruited me to be a proper space pilot. Real spaceships are easier to pilot than the virtual ones. Sounds a glamorous job, but it's not. I fly the same route in the same ship, carrying the same things, day after day, after day.

The other discs have all sorts of things they do for money: designing clothes, making water and food, hosting sports events (I'd much prefer to live there!), building spaceships, everything you can imagine. Some of it they want to sell and we have to – <u>have</u> to, it's the law – watch compulsorals where they advertise their things so that we buy their goods. It's a right pain, sometimes.

It's not an advantage being offline from compulsorals while I dock the ship; I'll get a double dose later to catch up. Today, that happens quicker than usual. As soon as I've landed, I'm delayed in my seat at the port by seven minutes to watch a compulsoral about cloned pets. They clone (make exact copies of) all sorts of animals these days – not just humans like me. I'm tempted by a rather cute Labrador puppy, but I don't have space in my living box.

I don't complain about the delay. There's no point. It's not as if I can do anything to stop them; they feed directly to a microchip inside that processor in my brain. Like everything else in this world, we're all joined up. One advantage is that the adverts are aimed at what I need and like. One big disadvantage is that they can be really, really boring!

I'm released by the compulsoral, and then I'm off at a sprint across the enormous landing ground, careful to avoid the docking spaces. I'm afraid that the ten percent for judgement allowed to the other pilots might be taken up landing a freighter on my head! They're not as good at it as me. No one is.

The moving public walkways are quick, but nowhere near as quick as I'd like. It's busy, too, which means I can't step out into the overtaking channel and get some added speed by running along the belt. I have to stand in line until my stop whisks me off into my chute.

"Blue top, red bottoms, blue trainers." I say the command as the chute deposits me in my living box. I say it because instructing by thinking what I want to wear gets me into all sorts of trouble. I can't make my mind up when it comes to clothes and, recently, I've had to be more direct in my commands, so I say them out loud. I've ended up in some weird outfits before. All sorts of daft colours. Once, I was trying to buy something to wear at the virtual beach and accidentally thought of a snowing holiday I'd seen on Disc 12.4. I ended up with ski boots and a thick coat! Hardly tropical beachwear.

I needn't have worried this time. The compulsorals have done their job. It's a new line and I've ordered and paid for the whole outfit on my way home, without my brain properly realising it.

"Cleanliness three," I say, as I enter my box. I don't fancy having the full 'scrub-up' today. Hair, armpits, face and teeth – that'll do. I'm through the wash-wardrobe within seconds, ready for Rose-Anne.

I sit down and try to kill time by watching some old 2-D Disney cartoons they're showing on the free-to-air channel, EarthNet. I have butterflies in my stomach: I really can't wait until I see Rose-Anne again.

And then I realise I've been fooled. Rose-Anne isn't really my girlfriend. Of course, she isn't. I'm too young and she's far too good for me anyway. The 'blink twice to pay now' details roll across my eyes and I hear her calm voice:

"Milo 8 – you have been experiencing a girlfriend-attracting compulsoral. Check out more cool clothes, video games, hairstyling, and sports equipment you can buy which will guarantee you get a girlfriend like me. These items are already on their way to you. Just blink twice to purchase."

I don't blink. I can't afford it!

There is more that I'm forced to listen to, but, in my mind, I've switched off. I should have known better, but the compulsorals are so convincing!

For the last twenty minutes – landing, running across the dock area, travelling the walkways, arriving in my box, watching the Disney cartoons, even watching the compulsoral about pets – I've been in a compulsoral. It felt

11

so real! They tap into your emotions, mess with your head and make you think you've been doing things you haven't been doing. It's hard to tell reality from the virtual world these days.

But I know for sure that I'm back in the real world when Rose-Anne's voice tails off and the bleak interior of the freighter cockpit is with me once more. I sigh as my ten percent of control is handed over to me, and I'm soon distracted by landing. The real landing this time.

There is a follow-up compulsoral when I'm down – shorter this time, but they're putting the pressure on for the girlfriend-attracting goods. I'm tempted, but I still won't buy.

In just over three years, when I'm sixteen, I'd be allowed to go to more places – other cool discs – where I could meet and hang out with older people, real people like Rose-Anne. Three years isn't that long to wait... but I know there's no point.

Why not?

Well, because I know something that no other human soul knows. Something so incredible and mind-blowing, you wouldn't believe it. No one would.

I see dots, brightly coloured swirling dots that look a lot like shoaling fish. These aren't the dots you might see, the phosphenes we all know about that appear if you stand up too quickly or stay in a dark room too long. My dots are special.

Shoal

Because my private display of shoaling fish is telling me something.

They tell me your future, our future, the future of mankind. The future of everything.

I have to tell you: it's not looking good.

It's not looking good at all...

Marcus

"Wake up, Marcus."

With a lot of effort, I open one eye. Someone's shouting at me from downstairs.

"Marcus?... Marcus!" It's Sean, my stepdad.

"I don't need to be awake." I call back. "It's Saturday."

"You do." Within a flash, he's at my door and poking his head through it. How do grownups do that? When they want you to do something, they use some weird Harry Potter kind of magic to transport instantaneously from one place to another so they can nag you face-to-face.

He frowns at the state of my room; jeans, T-shirts, socks, sweet wrappers and past editions of Kids Science Monthly are strewn about the floor. I don't get the usual telling-off, though, which tells me he must be in a hurry.

"Come on! You're taking Josh to football training. Your mum's been called into work and I'm going shopping with Matilda."

Being nearly a teenager and given more freedom and responsibility has its advantages. More time allowed for gaming, for example, or being allowed to go out on my own now and again. One of them, though, definitely isn't being responsible for taking snotty eight-year-old boys to football practice.

"You said you would take him," says Sean. "Now, move yourself, please. Josh needs to be there by nine."

I'm tired and I want to talk back to Sean, tell him he's not my father, that he shouldn't be ordering me around. I'm an adult – well, twelve going on thirteen would have been an adult in olden times – and I should be allowed to make my own decisions. There are lots of things I want to say, but I don't. Besides, Sean's not a bad bloke and is as close to being a father as I could hope for. The real one's not much good. I hardly ever see him these days.

I hear Matilda squawk as Sean leaves to concentrate on hurrying her along. My young half-sister I describe to friends as being a terror and a real pain. Actually, she's really cute. Sean gave up his job when she was born to look after her, making it easier for Mum to continue her career as editor of the local newspaper. Another plus point in his favour, I guess.

"Marcus, are you up?" Sean's back downstairs. I can tell he's getting anxious. The family weekly shop with a two-year-old toddler in tow is no fun at the best of times, but I remember now that he's in a particular rush to get away promptly. Mum was called in last night to deal with some big local story that's breaking. She doesn't normally work on a Saturday – it's Sean's golf morning, time with the lads –

but he's stepped in again, hoping she will be back in time for him to join them for the last nine holes.

"Coming!" I try to sound more cooperative, more helpful. 'More mature,' as Mum would say. "You go, I'll sort Josh."

"Thanks. You'll stay with him and bring him back in case your Mum's not back in time?"

Still in my pyjamas (Spiderman pyjamas which are too short for me and I would not be seen dead in outside of my house), I plod down the stairs and wave him on his way. "Go. I'll make sure he gets home."

I don't promise to stay with Josh during the practice. Watching a bunch of kids running around in different directions is not my idea of fun. I'll see if Stefan is free and hang out with him for a bit.

My phone pings, just as I'm putting my joggers on. It's a text from Stefan.

Have you heard the news?

Intrigued, I text back. *Wot news?*

Kids I know don't spend their time listening to or watching boring news programmes. At least Stefan and I don't, much to Mum's frustration.

Come to mine on your bike and I'll show you

BT in 10. Be there in ten minutes, our shortcut for saying we'll meet up as soon as possible.

BT in -10. Minus ten minutes. Looks like he's in a hurry but, in reality, I know that, even though the football ground is just a few minutes by bike, it will take time to get Josh out of the door, nag him to put his cycling helmet on, go back in the house for his boots, back out to the garage for our bikes, and then help him hunt around for a spare pair of shinpads at the ground because he will have forgotten those too.

I'm right, despite me asking if he had everything, but it's not far off the ten minutes that I said as I turn up to find Stefan is already waiting for me on his bike outside the bungalow that he shares with his elderly parents. They're Polish (though Stefan was born over here) and are the nicest people in the world. Always offering me food when I go round. Fat chance of that today, which is a shame because I skipped breakfast.

"You really not heard anything about this at all?" Stefan says as we cycle away. "Not even from your mum?"

"Heard what? I'm knackered. I went to bed about ten, just as Mum went out."

It's not the first time she's been called into the office to cover a story. I thought nothing of it when Sean mentioned it earlier.

"You're always knackered."

"Coz, I don't sleep well." I've been having more disturbed nights recently – not full-blown nightmares like I used to get with the shoals, just a bit more restless than usual. "Anyway, what's all this about? Where are we going?"

Stefan turns to grin at me before he accelerates off, and

all I can see is the back of his red helmet clashing badly with his ginger hair. His bike is quicker than mine – even with the show-off wheel spins and jumps he does on the way – and I struggle to keep up.

I imagine that, instead of being on our bikes, we're in our white Volkswagen Beetle, the old banger we've had for years. Mum can't bear to part with it and, to be honest, we all love it. With Mum's work only a fifteen-minute walk away, I'm hoping I will get free access to the *Love Bug* when I'm old enough and if they still have it then. It's already well over thirty years old and has a maximum speed of about fifty. No acceleration at all. Mum tried overtaking an electric scooter on a hill once and had to pull back in behind it. It's not the height of cool, but I don't care. It will give me more freedom.

I'm crazy about any car, if I'm honest. I watch those YouTube clips all the time from inside rally cars, amazed at how quick their reactions and gear changes are. Reckon I'd have no trouble taking the Love Bug out for a spin. Apart from the gears, it looks easy to drive.

I know Stefan's dead keen to learn to drive too. He wants to pass his test as soon as possible and buy himself a sportscar to show how super cool he is. He's already started to save up out of the money he gets from working after school and most weekends at the petrol station. I don't tell him he doesn't need a fast car to show that. He has this manner and confidence about him that kids at school – especially the girls – seem to like. Unlike me. They all think I'm a bit of a geek with all the science stuff I'm into.

"We'll turn right up here," he says over his shoulder.

"Towards the pits?" These are the clay pits formed by excavations from years ago. They're flooded now, and the small lakes and ponds are a local space for walks, fishing and the odd bit of scuba diving by the local club. It's also where Stefan and me like to hang out now and again.

"We might not be able to go all the way up," he adds.

I see why not as we make our way up the windy hill. Round the next bend are police cars, fire engines and ambulances blocking the road. A policeman waves us away.

"We'll go through the secret way," Stefan says. The secret way is not that secret. Most the local kids know about it, but it is off the beaten track. "Scoot off at the old tower and park the bikes out of sight behind it, then walk back up."

"Will you please tell me what is going on?"

"You know, for the son of a newspaper editor, you really are clueless about the news."

"I admit it, and so are you... normally. What's hooked you into this story?"

"What's hooked me in is the same as what is going to hook you in, young Marcus." He flashes that smile. "The aliens have landed!"

Shoal

We've dumped our bikes and are running uphill at pace now. The track is uneven, but we know it well enough to take small risks. Some of it passes high up, directly next to one of the ponds. There should be fences up on the edge to discourage kids from sliding down the banks. The weather's been dry but, if it was slippery, we would be especially careful around this section.

Rumours at school have it that a kid fell in a pond and drowned here in the 1980s. Over forty years later and they've still not bothered to make it safe. I should tell Mum – there must be a story in that about council failures. I won't, though; she would kill me if she knew what Stefan and I get up to around here.

I've tried to get Stefan to tell me more. All he says is that local people reported a bright object falling at speed into the area of the pits, and that the police were investigating.

"That doesn't mean it's an alien," I tell him.

"It doesn't mean that it isn't! Come on. If we cut across the ravine, we can circle round the back and watch from the other side of Lake Stefan. There won't be any coppers there and we'll get a good view. See what all the fuss is about."

Lake Stefan is the name he gave the biggest pond in the pits when we discovered this route as nine-year-olds. Like much of what Stefan says or does, it's stuck. It's the most popular lake because of its size and is the only one which you can get to by road. The road is on the opposite side to where we are now. As we near, it becomes clear by the distant thrum of engines that this might be where all the fuss that Stefan referred to is and the reason for the roadblock.

The last section as we approach Lake Stefan, we will need to take extra, extra care on. It's high up and there are all sorts of places where you can end up in trouble at the bottom of a steep fall. There's a lot of loose stones around too, particularly the closer to the edge you get.

Eventually, we come to an area above a small beach. We've caught a glimpse of the same beach from this angle before – and it's easy to see from the other side – but never been able to get onto it; even Stefan agrees it's far too a dangerous climb down. We snake our way through a gap in a bush, crouch behind a rock close to the cliff edge, and peer out from behind it.

The public car park opposite is packed with official-looking vans and cars, including a fire engine and a dozen or so police cars, all with their lights flashing. A couple of blokes are directing a huge lorry and trailer towards the lake edge. On the back sits a boat with a crane, a small version of the ones I've seen unloading goods at the docks. How on earth they got all that equipment up here on that windy road, I've no idea.

We realise as we look below onto the beach that the voices we could hear are a lot closer than we had thought.

An inflatable police dinghy sits half in and half out the water. I can just make out the tops of uniformed police officers' hats, a couple of men and a woman, and two, plainclothes officers or civilians.

"What are they looking at?" whispers Stefan. For once I'm a little in front of him and have a slightly better angle.

"I'm not sure."

There's a precipice overhanging the beach we could get to on our right. From it we'd get a better view from side-on without being seen if we stay low. But it's a scramble to get to and looks well dodgy. Stefan has pushed past me and is crawling onto it, flat on his stomach, even before we have a chance to discuss it.

"Stefan!" I hiss, but he's already off commando-style. Reluctantly, I follow and immediately regret it as my elbows scrape on the ground, and sticks and stones dig into my chest and thighs. Stefan is quickly in position, his head peering over the edge of what I realise, when I ease in beside him, is a fifteen or twenty-metre drop to the beach.

"Are we safe out on this bit?" I ask, dead scared that we aren't.

'Shush! Look. What is that?"

Nestled into a small crater in the mud hard up against the base of the cliff is a silver object, about the size of a car. Except it's not a car. Cars can't get round here, nor are they dome-shaped and, in my experience, they usually have wheels.

"Aliens!" Stefan hisses. "It's a spaceship."

"You can't be sure of that."

He turns his head towards me. "What is it then, and why else would the police be here?"

"Well..."

"Think about it. Your mum goes out late at night to investigate reports of lights in the sky. The area is closed off, loads of police hare up here, and now we see this!" I glance back at him. I always tease him that I can tell when he's excited because the freckles on his nose jump around. They don't, of course, but I can see the excitement in his eyes before he turns his attention back to below. "I need a better look."

"Don't. It's not safe." But his fingers are already pulling his bodyweight forward. He's barely moved, but already I can sense a shift in the ground beneath our stomachs.

"Careful," I say pointlessly. Careful is not a word Stefan understands.

"It's so shiny. Perfect looking." His voice is quiet, but even that small sound seems packed with danger as the precipice we're on groans under our weight.

"Move back," I urge. The excitement of what we've come here for is lost now as I start to panic.

"It's fine."

It's not fine. There's a crack and to our left a few stones

tumble towards the beach. If they hadn't already heard us from below, they'd know we were there now. There's another crack – louder this time – and I can feel the whole lot beginning to go. Stefan knows it too, as more of the ground breaks up. Both of us furiously scramble back, a flurry of arms and legs trying to stop something that gravity is the master of now.

It's too late and my stomach lurches as we start to fall. Desperately, I reach out, clasping at what turns out to be a lot of falling rocks and even more thin air. Then, the world turns upside down as we tumble in slow motion.

The swooping shoals of fish appear and quickly disappear across my eye line as I scream out.

But I scream not only because I'm falling. I scream because I suddenly realise something I had missed all my life: the dots I've been seeing at nighttime since I was young are not shoals of fish, or even the phosphenes the scientists say we all get.

These are stars – real stars – and they're not just swirling around randomly.

They're running away from something.

No wonder I have nightmares!

Milo

Those dots I mentioned that I've seen, like shoals of fish… they're not dots or phosphenes. Neither are they shoals of fish.

They are stars – actual stars – and they're not just swirling around randomly. They're running away from something.

How do I know? Well, this might be hard to believe, but I've been visited by an alien. Yep, a real alien, a being not from the discs that orbit our planet, not from anywhere near here.

Officially, aliens don't exist. Sure, there were loads of sightings on Earth when humans lived down there, but since we've been up here, living on the discs, it's all gone quiet on that front. People say that when humans properly reach the stars, we'll find out for sure. Well, I can save them a lot of time and bother; aliens exist alright. One of them's been inside my living box to talk to me.

She – she sounds like a 'she' – has an unusual way of talking. Quite slow, as if she's thinking hard about what she's saying before saying it. And she's not how you might imagine your standard-looking alien might look… whatever that might be. She's… how can I describe it?... Different. Different in lots of ways.

So far, I've kept all this to myself. People would laugh if I told them I'd had visits from an alien. But that's not the reason I've not told anyone. I wouldn't, anyway; there's not much point.

Why isn't there? Well, because this alien has been showing and explaining a few things to me.

I was right; there's no point to anything.

Marcus

The next two months are confusing. I'm at the local hospital – St Cuthbert's – recovering from three cracked ribs, a punctured lung, a broken ankle, a broken wrist and a whole heap of cuts and bruises. Two months! Each time I think they will send me home, something else comes up as a problem.

Pneumonia is the latest thing, but I've also had other infections. It's been a truly horrendous time, made worse by the fact that they won't tell me anything about Stefan and how he is. I'm assuming he isn't dead, otherwise, someone would have told me by now, but each time I ask, the answer is the same: "Don't worry yourself, Marcus. Concentrate on getting better." It's like it's been pre-programmed into every single visitor, nurse, doctor, social worker and – yes – police officer.

There's been a police investigation into what happened. It's almost like they think we pushed each other, or something. Or if it was some kind of dare to jump off. Madness! I have a theory that they've been trying to divert attention away from what was really going on there.

The idea of aliens and that strange silver object we saw... well, it's all gone suspiciously quiet.

It's been decided, in the end, that our fall was an accident. On the upside, perhaps the council will do something about the fences and safety up there now.

It's been hard for me to see Mum so upset when she comes to visit me. For much of the time, I've been out of it. But when I've been more alert, I can see then that she's been through hell worrying about me. Sean's played a blinder supporting her and keeping the house and family going. He's been great with me too. He visits every day and keeps me entertained with games and by bringing along Matilda. I might have to start calling him "Dad" soon. Even Snotface Joshua has been good, although I've told him not to skip any more football practices just to visit me. I don't want him to miss out on a regular team place. (To give him credit, he is one of the few kids in his team who is normally facing the right way in games).

No sign of my real dad. I try not to let it bother me... but it does.

I finally get news that I'm well enough to be sent home, provided the ear, nose and throat doctor is prepared to sign me off. She pays me a visit and tells me that I'm free to leave, but I have to stay indoors for a couple of weeks and mustn't go off chasing mysterious aliens that don't exist. I can go back to school as soon as the summer holidays are over in three weeks.

Everyone is very kind and supportive, but I'm not sure I

can just go back to school as if nothing has happened. Things have changed. I've changed. How exactly, I'm not too sure yet.

Two massive events happening at the same time: what looked like a spaceship crashing near where I live, and the clear message I got as I fell from the cliff that the stars were leaving. If that last thing is true, surely it means it's the end of everything.

I'm thinking about that when I hear a knock at the door. (One plus point of catching pneumonia is that they gave me my own room). The nurse has already helped me get my things together, I'm dressed, ready to go, and sitting in my chair. I've texted Sean so I know it can't be him at the door; he'll be here in an hour after he's picked up Matilda from playgroup. No one normally knocks, so I look up, surprised.

There's a girl standing there. I say that she's a girl; it's confusing because she's young-looking but she's wearing a white coat and has a stethoscope around her neck. Mum's always saying that police officers look younger every day. Maybe the same goes for medical staff.

"I've already seen the throat doctor," I say. "Are you another doctor?"

"Do I look like one?" Her voice sounds a bit mechanical, like every word has been thought about before it has come out of her mouth. A little slow and unnatural. She doesn't have an accent so I can't put it down to her being from another country.

"Yes... no... I don't know. You're dressed like a doctor."

I break into a short coughing fit and grab a tissue from the table, slightly embarrassed by the fact that a bit of green snot is on my hand.

"I'm here to talk about your nightmares."

Since the fall off the cliff, the nightmares have come back... with a vengeance. Those stars...

"So, you're a psychiatrist then?" – A head doctor – "I saw one of those a few weeks back, I think."

I stop, unsure if I did or not. I remember mentioning to someone about not being able to sleep well, but maybe it wasn't a psychiatrist. Whoever it was, they didn't help. I was given sleeping pills which I've stopped taking because I end up sleeping more, the result of which is more time for nightmares.

"No, not a..." She pauses and her eyes look up. It's like she's practising the word in her head before she says it. "... a psychiatrist." It's said perfectly well, but it's weird. She's weird. Pretty, I notice, but weird. She repeats herself. "I'm here to talk about your nightmares."

I'm not comfortable. Something's not right here. There's a cord to pull for assistance, but it's out of reach on the other side of the bed. I curse myself for not having it near me. I normally do, but I guess I was thinking I wouldn't need it anymore.

Shoal

She's closed the door now and is standing at the end of the bed, staring at me. She looks a couple of years older than me – fourteen or fifteen, maybe – quite small. If I stood up, I reckon I'd have a good five or six inches on her. I want to do precisely that but I can't. Too tired.

"Tell me about the nightmares... please." That pause again and the eyes flicking up before the word "please". It's like something is telling her that if she adds that word on at the end, I'm more likely to respond. I don't. She takes a step towards me and stops.

I'm getting seriously worried now. I want to shout out, yet I'm also curious. All of a sudden, she holds a hand up and I'm drawn into looking at her palm. "Tell me, please." There's a red disc in the middle, not stuck to it but detached, floating on top and slightly to the front.

While I watch, it starts to get bigger and, as it does, I can see that it's rotating. It's no longer red but is now hundreds of different colours and shades. It continues to increase in size and now I can make out individual dots, like my dots. But these don't move across from side to side and up and down like mine; these ones rotate. I've seen something like this before, many times on TV, and in my science books and magazines. They are galaxies – spirals made up of millions and billions of stars, all clustered together, spinning round and round, a kaleidoscope of wonder and brilliance.

I can no longer see her hand or face now; they're covered

by the display in front of me. I'm suddenly aware of a movement and realise that she's slowly stepping back and releasing the disc which is the size of a basketball now. As she pulls away, my stomach lurches, and my view suddenly changes. It's no longer 2D, not even 3D but something else, something I can't explain. Despite the wonder of it, I have a deep-down feeling of dread. It's giving me the same feeling I've been having most nights in my nightmares. The same feeling I had as a young kid when they were really bad.

"Tell me about the nightmares, Marcus."

I can hear her voice, soft and gentle, encouraging me to talk, but I'm not ready to answer yet. I'm sucked into the galaxies, spinning with them, feeling their scorching heat, blinded by their bright cores, pulled in by their gravity. I can smell each and every gas within each star. They all pass through my lungs: hydrogen, helium, oxygen, nitrogen. The heavier elements bounce off of me as I pass by – carbon, iron, uranium, gold – before whole systems explode in a supernova. I watch new stars and galaxies being born. I see tiny planets, moons, comets, and rocks hurtling through space. They are small compared to the stars but I feel their strength, their size compared to me. I'm tiny, not important. I move at frightening speed; slow, stop, then move again. I'm floating, dancing, jumping, running, crawling. Backwards, forwards, up, down, in and out, falling and soaring up high. Every possible movement, all at the same time. I feel cold, so cold — colder than anything I can imagine. But on the inside, I'm burning. I am fire. I am ice. I am... everything.

The dread I felt to start with, goes, and for a while it's bliss. Happiness surges through me until... it all stops. And then it's gone.

She's there, still, at the end of the bed, staring at me, waiting for a response. I take a deep breath and hold her gaze for a second. I'm surprised by how calm I feel. It's like a weight has been lifted from my shoulders. Because, in that moment, I knew I could do what I could never do as a child when I had the nightmares. I can do what I couldn't do to Mum and Sean when I was younger. I can do what I could never do to myself.

I can describe the nightmares.

I don't need to think about what I'm going to say; it just comes out: "The nightmares are like that, but the opposite."

She waits again before responding. "The opposite?" One eyebrow goes up as if it's a question, but she gets the stress in the sentence wrong and her voice goes down.

"Yes, the opposite."

"Explain."

I'm surprised she doesn't understand. "The opposite to all that is..." She is patient, waiting for me. "The opposite to all that is... nothing. There's nothing. There will be nothing."

"Is it blackness." The attempted question comes out as a statement again. It doesn't matter because she is wrong.

"No, not blackness. Blackness is something. This is nothing."

She nods her understanding.

"When?"

I close my eyes and I see my shoals of fish – the stars – streaming past. I have no control over the next words that come out of my mouth. "Soon. Very soon. When the stars have all left."

She nods again and leaves. It's then that I properly understand the nightmares I've been having.

The fish – the stars – are just part of it. When they go, there will be nothing.

Nothing surely means that it's the end of everything.

The end of everything... that's gotta be worth screaming about.

So, that's exactly what I do.

Milo

The last time she – the alien – visited me was three months ago. She said she would be back with more information but didn't say when. Since then, I've been trying to carry on with my job as a freighter pilot, doing my pickups from Mars. I'm told they've nearly got out everything they can from the Hellas basin, so I don't know how much longer I'll be working there.

Not that it matters.

Every day's the same: I get up, eat, leave my box, go to my freighter, fly out, bring a load of rocks and metal back, get out of my freighter, go to my box, eat, sleep. Oh, and I experience compulsorals. Can't miss them! Then I get to do it all over again. Not much of a life for a twelve going on thirteen-year-old.

If I'm honest, it wasn't that great before the alien visited.

Because we are clones and don't have biological mothers, we are given a nursery mother who is supposed to look after us. Supposed to. I hardly ever see mine. But, in a rare moment of interest in my life, she said that becoming the youngest ever freighter pilot at the age of eleven wouldn't be as glamorous as I hoped it might be. She's wrong about a lot of things, but she was right about that.

It was fun to start with. I swaggered around in my fancy blue and grey uniform, thinking I was the coolest kid on the disc. I believed everyone was looking at me and thinking the same, until I realised that no one ever blinked an eye. I hoped space freighting would keep me interested, at least until I had done enough hours to go for the chance to earn my stellar wings. That's what I want to do – wanted to do – become a stellar cadet and then a pilot, travel around in really fast rockets and see the universe, or the dozen or so stars we can get to in our tiny corner of the Milky Way. The hope of doing that kept me going.

Not now. It's not worth spending any time or effort.

The alien said I should carry on as if nothing was wrong, but that's hard when you know what I know. Carrying that around is a massive stress, though I try to control it during the day.

It's at night when I go to sleep that it all becomes very tricky.

I used to quite enjoy my shoals of colourful fish. I could close my eyes and watch them pass by; streams of flickering lights flowing past, again and again and again. But she took that peaceful place away from me by making me realise what they really were and where they were heading.

Now, I have nowhere to go. No hopes, no dreams, just the reality of living on a freighter disc, pointlessly transporting minerals from one dead planet to the edges of

another, until the end of everything.
　The end of everything… and I know it's going to happen.
　Soon.
　I wish I'd never be cloned.

Marcus

It's two weeks after being discharged and I'm feeling much better. No sign of pneumonia and my injuries are healing nicely. This has made me think that perhaps Little Miss Weird in the hospital does not, and did not, ever exist.

I was weak then, wasn't I? Still ill, emotional and, judging by what the nurse said when he rushed in after I screamed, all on my own. Their station is right outside my room and they had seen no one go in or come out. The whole episode was too strange to be anything other than another one of my nightmares.

I'm happy with that explanation; it's easy to accept. Nothing to see here! Nothing happened.

I found out as soon as I got home why everyone had been so careful about telling me how Stefan was. Mum sat me down and told me that it was still touch and go whether he was going to live or not. It shook me up, particularly on the back of my experience with the girl and her box of tricks. But that very same evening, we got news that Stefan had come out of the coma he had been in since the fall and was, for the first time sitting up in bed. The doctors described it officially as "unexpected, but a very welcome development." Unofficially, Stefan tells me later, he had heard one nurse say they were all gobsmacked. They had not expected him to live.

Stefan had suffered the worst of our combined injury count, certainly in terms of how seriously hurt we both were. He had gone over the edge fractionally before me, resulting in part of me landing on part of him. He got serious head injuries, many broken ribs and damage to one of his kidneys. That last injury was down to how I fell on top of his side, partly crushing him. One of the policemen had said that the positions where we both landed were such that, had Stefan not got there first, I would likely have cracked my head on a rock. Without Stefan underneath me, I might've been killed.

Now as I sit by his bed, him having just said to me that I should be forever in his debt for saving his life, I have just answered by saying that he is usually so full of hot air that I was disappointed he hadn't floated down, carrying me with him.

"Don't. It hurts my ribs when I laugh!" he says.

It's good to see my friend looking well. I hadn't realised how much I'd missed hanging out with him. You take these things for granted. We sit there for a few minutes not saying anything, intent, instead, on tucking into the grapes that I wasn't strictly supposed to bring in. New hygiene rules, apparently.

Eventually, Stefan breaks the silence. "So, what of the

Shoal

alien invasion, then? What do you think that metal thing was that we saw at the pits?"

Since I'd got home, I had almost forgotten about the silver object on the beach. How could I have done that? Maybe worrying about Stefan and my own health had been my focus, so much so that I had given little thought as to why we had gone up to the pits in the first place.

"I heard that your Mum's newspaper reported the flashing lights as probably being some sort of large drone going wrong." He goes all serious for a moment. "That was no drone we saw by the lake."

"Is that why you decided to take a closer look by jumping off?"

"I didn't jump off!" He laughs again, holding his side this time. "Seriously though, Marcus, that wasn't a drone. It was the wrong shape and size. And much too big."

The view of the cylinder from above jumps into my brain. He's right. It was like no flying machine I had ever seen. I feel a sudden lurch in my stomach; a tiny taste of the feelings I get in the nightmares. It bothers me and I go quiet as I try to work out what it means. To get my attention, Stefan gives the plaster around my wrist a solid tap.

"Ow!" It doesn't hurt, but I'm not going to tell him that.

"Talk to me, you ape. What was it?"

"I don't know. I agree with you that it wasn't a drone, but I can't say what it was."

"I think I saw some sort of wing on it, but that looked all crumpled up. Peculiar markings, too. I reckon from the angle it was at that it had landed in the lake and then skimmed across to the beachy bit."

"That's impossible. It would have had to come in on a flat flight path to do that. The lake's not big enough, and remember, it's surrounded by high sides nearly all the way around. Besides, the reports said that there was a falling object, not a flying object. Whatever it is, it probably came down straight onto the lake."

"So?" He gives me an expectant look. He's waiting for me to come up with a theory. But I haven't got one. Not one that makes any sense.

Rather reluctantly, my thoughts turn back to that hour before I was discharged and the visit from the strange girl. Did it happen after all? Surely not. But she showed me something amazing... so fantastic that part of me wants to believe it was real, apart from the awful final part with the stars leaving. I don't want to go down this route, but Stefan, as is often the case, has got me thinking. Could what I think I witnessed with the girl – no, not witnessed, actually became part of – really have taken place? Could the girl who came to my room be some sort of alien who landed by the lake in a spaceship and then came to see me disguised as a doctor? That's crazy, isn't it?

I have a sudden need to tell Stefan everything. Stefan

knows I've had problems with my nightmares – even if he doesn't know exactly what they're like – and is sympathetic, despite taking the mickey too. But will he be so understanding this time?

"Come on," he says. "Out with it. I know you; you're hiding something from me."

"Well..."

"Marcus, there's nothing better to do in here. You might as well talk."

So, I do. I tell him about the shoals of fish and I tell him about the girl and her ability to show me the universe, how I felt during it, and how beautiful it was. I tell him how afterwards I had the same feeling of emptiness and despair that I used to get in my nightmares. I stop short of telling him what the shoals of fish are. I can't face that just yet.

When I finish, he doesn't laugh like I thought he might. Instead, he just looks at me strangely. "What did this person look like?" I describe her the best I can. "Young, you say? Good-looking?"

"Yes... I guess you could say she was good-looking."

"Spoke carefully all the time? One eyebrow went up now and again?"

"Yes! How did you know?" I had not mentioned those things.

"I'm sure someone like that came to see me. When I came out of my coma, she was there by my bed. I thought it was a doctor."

Not a dream then. Real. "What did she say?"

"She said that I was going to be alright now. That I was going to live."

"Did she say anything else?"

"Not much." Stefan's brow wrinkles as he tries to recall something. "Hang on, yes... I remember now because of the strange way she said it. She said something like, 'He must survive. It is very important.' That might not be it exactly and there might have been more, but that was the gist of it. I thought she was talking about me surviving, but now I think about it, she definitely said 'he' rather than 'you' as in meaning me."

"He must survive," I repeat it a couple of times. "Who? Who is she talking about?"

"Isn't it obvious? It's you, you big lump."

"Me?"

"Yes, of course! I didn't see any magical universe show or anything. You did. She came to show you."

"Now, wait a minute. What are you suggesting here? That we've both been visited by an alien?"

"Marcus, think about it. A spacecraft lands, we get hurt, we both meet the same strange girl. You experience something magical and within hours, maybe minutes of that, I'm cured."

"You think she made you better?"

"They told my mum and dad they thought I was going to die." It's the first time I've seen Stefan react to anything with any real emotion. There is a definite tear in his eye. "My poor old dad said he had given up. I get a visit from this girl and then I'm suddenly out of my coma and on the road to recovery. You've got to admit that it is a bit freaky."

I try to grasp hold of what can be the only possible explanation. "We both might have been dreaming."

"About the same person? Is that what you really believe? It isn't, is it?" As usual, Stefan has shown how well he knows me.

I can't answer, at first. A dream is what I want to believe, but deep down I know that it wasn't that. The thought makes me go cold. Stefan notices it.

"What is it?"

"I'm afraid, Stefan. I'm afraid of what that girl has shown me. I got a glimpse of a universe, an incredible place, full of wonderful things. A place where you and I exist and a place where other life exists."

"That's amazing, then, isn't it?"

"Yes, but there's more. Those dreams I've mentioned about shoals of fish."

"Yeah?"

"After that strange experience in hospital, I'm even more sure that my nightmares are connected."

Stefan shifts from side to side in an effort to sit himself

up more. "Go on."

I finally tell him more about my shoals of fish, what they look like, how they move and... and I want to say something else that happened. That feeling at the end of the girl's visit. Something horrible that made me scream out. The thing that makes the nightmares so nightmarish. But just like with Mum and Dad years ago, I can't find the right words to explain what it is, how it makes me feel.

Stefan suddenly blurts out: "I've remembered what she said to me now."

"He must survive. It's very important. You told me."

"She said something else, too. She said, 'It is our only chance.' He – you – must survive. It is very important. It's our only chance. Marcus, what did she mean? What's our only chance? What's going to happen?"

I feel sick. I don't want to say what those fish really are, but I know I must because this secret is already partly out of its box. If there is a chance to survive, I realise that the lid has to be fully lifted now. I mutter the words quietly: "The stars are leaving, Stefan."

"Leaving?"

"The shoals of fish I see are actually stars, and I see all of them leaving."

He goes pale. "Leaving for where?"

I can barely say anything. Eventually, I stutter, "I don't know."

"Well, this alien obviously thinks you can do something about it." He sits up a little, moulding his pale face into a look of determination.

"Me? How?" *He must survive. It is very important. It's our only chance.* Could Stefan be right? Can I do something about it? Can I stop the stars leaving? I look down again: the horror and the responsibility I feel are suddenly too much.

My feeling of doom is violently interrupted by a shriek and my heart skips a beat. Until I realise that it's Stefan, laughing. I stare at him in amazement, but he just stares back. All of the paleness has gone and he is beaming broadly. "You're the main man and I've been cured so that I can help."

"What?"

"That girl wants me to guide and protect you so you can save the stars. Stop them leaving." He starts to unplug a tube that's running into his arm.

"What are you doing? You can't do that. Stop!" I stand up, concerned that he's going to put back his recovery if he carries on like this. "You're in hospital for a reason, still. Stefan, the doctors said you need more time. Leave that alone!"

I try to coax him back onto his pillow, but he's unstoppable now. He throws back the sheets and swings his legs around. "I'm fine. Come on; help me out of this bed."

"No!"

"Marcus..." He coughs then changes his tone so it sounds just like the man in the voiceover for the Avengers film. "The universe in is trouble... and there's only one person..." he coughs again as his voice breaks and goes up before he goes deep again, "persons... correction, two people... ahem... two persons, who can save it. We are those two people-persons."

Before I realise what's happening, he has unplugged all the tubes, is dressed, and we are sneaking our way out of the hospital, out towards the taxi rank.

"And your plan is...?" I ask, looking about nervously. I'm expecting several beefy doctors in white coats to jump out any second and haul us back inside.

"We go back to the pits and take a good look around. There might be clues or maybe the aliens might still be there."

"But..."

"We'll get a taxi."

"No taxi driver will take two boys our age up there without an adult. They'll be suspicious."

He grabs my good arm and we stop. "You're right. And neither of us is in a fit state to cycle up. A taxi will take us back to your house, though."

"And then what?"

"We drive up."

"Drive up? How...?"

"You've always been crazy about driving that clapped-out old Beetle. Now's your chance. Is anyone at home?"

I stare at him, flabbergasted. "No. Mum's at work, Big-Snotface is in school and Mini-Snotface is with Sean visiting his parents. You say that you want me to drive?"

"You can do it."

"It's illegal. We'll get into trouble. *I'll* get into trouble."

"Is that as important as trying to stop the universe being destroyed?"

He doesn't wait for an answer but sets off for the first taxi in the rank. In a daze, I follow and clamber in the back of a taxi behind him. He's already giving the driver my home address and explaining that his mum asked us to make our own way back from visiting his granddad in hospital.

He then lowers his tone and whispers to me, "I don't suppose that alien girl gave you any cash to pay for the taxi, did she?"

Milo

I said the alien was different. 'Different' hardly does justice to it.

She is what I can only describe as a gloopy, yellow and green spinning mass, about the size of my fist. Not the standard-looking alien (whatever you thought that might look like). A couple of visits, just to shake me up by telling me the end of the universe is near, and then I hear nothing.

Well, the gloopy thing, after nearly four months, is finally back.

"It's you again," I say as cooly as I can, pretending like I don't care.

"Yes."

I do care, of course. But I'm also a little fed up. "What do you want?"

"We want you."

"We?" This is new. "There's more than one of you?"

"Yes. Many.

"How many?"

"Many. It was one, now we are many. I speak for the many."

She has suddenly become *They*, it seems. It doesn't make things any less weird. It's the same gloopy, yellow and green spinning mass, about the size of my fist, but now it seems it's lots of aliens, all rolled up into one gloopy, yellow and green spinning mass, about the size of my fist.

"You said that you want me. What do you mean that you want me?" I'm suddenly very angry. "You appear out of nowhere, talk to me about the universe being about to explode or finish or something, and then I don't see you for ages. You worry me sick and now you say you want me."

"We want you for an important task. You are special."

"Special? Well, if you think a twelve-year-old freighter pilot is special, then I'm your boy! I can't think what makes me special, other than flying big ships, buying things that I don't need, and not being able to attract a proper girlfriend."

There's a pause as the alien/aliens think that one through. Finally, they say: *"It is not your ability to fly, buying things that you don't need, and not being able to attract a proper girlfriend that we want."*

"What is it then?" I have to keep asking lots of questions to get information. Just like the compulsorals, it seems, nothing's given away for free.

"You were shown what is happening to the stars. You remember?"

"Of course, I remember." How could I forget?

"You can help. That's why we want you."

"You make no sense!" I've got lots of questions which I

want an answer to, but they don't seem to understand that. "You need to tell me, now, what you want of me." I try – badly – to sound like I'm in charge.

"It will become clear. We have little time. You may ask one question before we go."

"Go where?"

"You will see. That was your one question."

I don't even have a chance to say how unfair that was before I'm turned inside out and transported at what feels like a million miles an hour into a chute, out through some vent in the disc I call home, and deposited into space.

In the blink of an eye, the dead planet that humans used to call Earth is a tiny blue dot. I barely have time to wave to Neptune before I've left the solar system and am heading into unknown stellar territory.

It would be quite a ride, one I've dreamed of taking many times, if I didn't feel so incredibly sick...

Marcus

The Love Bug is harder to drive than Mum makes it look. I quickly find out that I'm no rally driver either, that's for sure.

I understand the theory of how to do it, but actually doing it is another thing. I know which pedals are the clutch, brake and accelerator, and I understand that you need to start in first gear and gradually go through the gears as you pull away, just like on a bike. What I'm struggling with is how to do all that at the same time, and make sure I don't crash into anything. Having one arm in plaster is not making it any easier – Stefan has to hold the wheel when I change gear – nor is having him constantly shouting in my ear to be careful.

The turnoff to the pits is only a mile away, thank goodness, but it takes us nearly ten minutes with my regular stalling of the engine and somewhat wobbly steering. Somehow, we get there without mowing anyone down or running into the police, and with me only having to threaten Stefan twice that my plastered arm would be used as a weapon unless he kept his big mouth closed.

I breathe a sigh of relief as we start to chug up the hill towards the pits. The chances of meeting any traffic on this road are very slim and Stefan assures me the police will be long gone. One thing for sure is that we wouldn't be able to outrun anyone in this thing, not uphill, anyway.

There's a crunch that makes me wince and we jolt forward as I accidentally go from third into first gear. Stefan lets out a quiet moan and holds his head.

"Are you okay to be doing all this?" I ask to stop him having a go at me again. "Perhaps you should be back in hospital."

"I'm fine," he says. "Just keep going. We're nearly at the tower." This is where we left our bikes what seems like a lifetime ago, and I see it now as we round the bend. "We'll go right to the top to the car park; it'll save the walk."

"Are you certain there won't be any police? If that was an alien spaceship, surely, they would have realised that by now and cordoned off the area."

"That's possible, but I doubt it. They've probably taken it away for examination. It was over two months ago. Why would they shut all the area off still?"

"To check the area for alie... for unusual things," I add hurriedly.

"Ahh! So, you do admit it was an alien spaceship?"

I glance sideways and catch a glimpse of his smirk, before realising we're on a bend and it would be better if I kept my eyes on the road. I say nothing and we spend the rest of the journey in silence. I prefer it that way so I can concentrate on driving. Full respect for Mum and Sean for making this driving lark look so simple.

Eventually, after a few more dodgy moments and more clunky gear changes, we reach the top. Stefan is right; there are no police around. No army, no anyone, in fact. The road doesn't go any further, so I pull into the small car park. I have a choice of more than fifty free spaces where I want to leave the car but still manage to go over the white lines and leave it at a wonk. There is a loud creak as I pull the handbrake up.

"Nice drive, Lewis Hamilton."

I choose to ignore Stefan's sarcastic comment. After all, this wasn't my idea.

Some trails lead off towards the various lakes and ponds, but we head for the main lake where we saw the spacecraft, just a short walk on the other side of the car park.

It's getting a little dark, I notice. I check my watch and see that it's just gone two o'clock. There are plenty of summer hours left in the day and there aren't many clouds in the sky, which leaves me a little confused as to why it feels like it's so much later. I can see Stefan has noticed it too as he is looking around him and squinting a little as we walk. I shiver, regretting my decision to wear shorts and a T-shirt that morning. It wasn't a bad choice then; it was twenty-two degrees when I caught the bus to the hospital. Stefan has a T-shirt on too. He rubs his bare upper arms and even goes so far as to blow into his hands. The temperature is dropping quickly. At least he has joggers on.

"It's the lake," he explains. "It's always cooler by water." I can hear the doubt in his voice and I try to answer, but my teeth have started to chatter now. I suddenly start to worry if it's the pneumonia on its way back.

We press on and are soon at the lake's edge. Despite the gloom, we can see the small beach on the other side of the lake where the spacecraft was. It's not there now. My eyes are drawn upwards to the cliff where we fell. It's about fifty or sixty metres away, but even from here it looks a long way down. I feel my stomach tighten a little as I think about how much worse our injuries could have been. Strictly, Stefan shouldn't even be alive, let alone walking around. Maybe neither of us should be. People don't normally survive falling from such a height.

There are picnic tables and benches scattered around this side of the lake. A small jetty is over to our right with a dozen or so red-bottomed rowing boats on the sandy grass nearby, turned upside down. They look like the enormous sunburnt stomachs of men buried in the sand on a beach. To our left is a small play area which wasn't here last time I came to this side a year or so ago. Both Snotfaces would like playing on that.

A thought strikes me: "Isn't it a bit strange that no one is up here taking advantage of the school holidays and the nice weather?"

"What nice weather? I'm freezing!" Stefan's shaking more than me now.

"This place is normally busy at this time of year. We didn't see one car on our way up, and the car park's empty."

Stefan grunts, apparently not impressed by my observation. He seems distracted. "Didn't there used to be a path that went around the lake?"

"I think so. You go past the boats and it starts behind that line of bushes." I point and he follows the direction of my hand. "I don't know if it goes all the way round or off towards one of the other lakes."

"It's worth a go," he says. "Hopefully, it will get us to the beach. I think we should go look to see if there is any sign that our spaceship was there."

I doubt there will be, but we need to check it out. That's why we've come up here. I'm keen to get moving again, hoping that a brisk walk will warm me up a little.

"Keep an eye out for any signs of aliens," Stefan says.

"Signs of aliens?" I mutter under my breath as we head towards the path. I look up at the still very blue, bright sky with the sun beating down before looking around the lake again. Impossibly, it's got even darker down here. And colder.

I hate to admit it, but it all feels pretty alien to me.

The path winds its way around through thick bushes and

trees, one of those well-worn paths that people have traipsed along for years. There are spots where, if it had not been so hot and dry recently, it would be muddy, so it's easy enough today to navigate. Now and then, we come across signs of human activity: left-behind plastic Coke bottles and crisp packets; a dodgy swing made out of a piece of wood dangling from a straggly rope on a tree branch; a bunch of upright sticks tied at the top to form a tepee shape, a den of some sort; an old car tyre dumped into a bush. I can see the potential for another article for Mum and her newspaper here about the lack of respect shown by people in the countryside. I wonder, briefly, what Mum really thought of the alien sighting – it had never occurred to me to ask. Or perhaps I was too scared to in case I didn't like the answer.

Stefan is ten or so paces in front of me. He is limping slightly and holding his side. I'm not feeling great either. Two months of virtually no activity is having its effect on me. I'm tired, cold and worried about going off with Mum's car.

Somehow, in a very short space of time, we have lost sight of the lake. I think it's over to the right through the bushes and trees, but it's hard to tell. I try to convince myself that the darkening atmosphere around us is a result of my darkening mood. However, this path is going nowhere. And neither are we. We need to stop this ridiculous wild-goose chase.

I call out to Stefan: "Let's go home. This is a waste of

time. We should get back before anyone notices the car is gone."

I get no answer. He just limps on ahead.

"Stefan?... Stefan, wait!"

He gets like this sometimes: all moody and stroppy.

Annoyed with his stubbornness, I quicken my pace to catch up with him. Incredibly, without turning round, he has sped up too. I yell out to him again but it's pointless; he just carries on regardless. We're more or less running now and I can't make any ground on him. I've not exercised anything like this since the fall and I'm struggling to catch my breath.

Up ahead, I can see that the path splits. I'm expecting Stefan to stop here to choose which way to go but he just ploughs on, taking the left-hand route. I've no clue how far away from the lake we are now, but my instinct tells me that this route will take us even further away. I try to call out, however my lungs don't have the strength in them. It comes out as a gasp and a splutter, and I have to stop.

There's a fallen tree trunk nearby and I collapse onto it, panting heavily with my arms across my knees and my head down between them. I feel sick and a little bit panicky as I struggle to get my breath back. They taught me in the hospital to just concentrate on my breathing if I started to feel like this, so I do that now.

I focus on a point on the ground — a brown and white stone — and tell myself that the physical feelings I am experiencing are just my body trying to put things right. It helps and gradually I start to feel more in control.

When I feel a little better, I turn my attention back to our situation and lift my head to look around. It's no darker than it was, but it is such an odd experience. I can still make out the brightness of the sky high above, a blue and white carpet of light sitting on top of me. I imagine it's a bit like being a diver deep underwater, looking up through the surface to the sky above. It's eerie.

On the plus side, after all that running, I no longer feel cold.

There's still no sign of Stefan. I suddenly feel angry with him for getting me into this position, and it goes through my mind that maybe I should just leave him up here if he's going to be so stupid. I reach into my front pocket for my phone. I'll text him and tell him to come back straight away, otherwise I will leave without him.

I type in my passcode and then sigh – no bars mean no signal. Cursing under my breath, I walk up a little further in search of a better reception, hoping that Stefan has come to his senses and stopped.

He has. Stopped that is. There's no way to tell if he's come to his senses, though, because he has his eyes firmly shut... and he's floating upside down inside a green circular ring.

I rush towards him, calling his name, but no sound comes

out. I keep shouting but I know I'm making no noise. The harder I try, the harder it seems. I'm getting no closer either. It's like those dreams you have where you're desperately trying to run away or towards something, but your legs and arms won't get you anywhere.

Then it stops being the dreams everyone has... and becomes the nightmares I have.

I get a quick glimpse of my shoals of fish as they rush by before darkness descends and Stefan is no longer there.

And then the darkness goes too... and there is nothing.

Part 2 – To the Edge

Milo

I hear a voice: "Milo 8. Milo 8." It's faint. Female. Familiar.

It speaks again: "Milo 8. Are you okay?"

Very familiar. Sounds a bit like Rose-Anne. She repeats the question: "Are you okay?"

It's a good question – am I okay? I think I am but it's hard to tell. I can't feel anything much. I try to answer, but no words come out. It looks like she's understood that I'm having problems speaking because she says simply: "You are okay. I can confirm."

I grunt. That didn't work either. I don't think I can make any sort of noise at all.

I blink and then I'm suddenly surrounded by stars, rushing past at speeds that I'm not used to at all in my old freighter. My insides still feel like they are on the outside. I close them again. It's too much.

I want to ask some questions, but, again, my voice just won't have it.

"Think it."

Since I have no idea where my mouth is or how to use it

properly, that seems like a good plan. With some effort, I manage to think the words I want to say. They come out in a rush: "What's happening? Where am I? What... where... what... where...what...?"

"Do not worry," the voice that sounds like Rose-Anne says. "You are safe... for now." I don't like the way she adds that last bit. "You will soon become fully operational." Fully operational? What am I – a cleaning bot? "We are just making final temporal adjustments and then you will be fully operational."

Temporal adjustments...? Temporal means time and everyone knows that you can't mess around with that. Believe me: our scientists have seriously looked at ways to turn back the clock to try to stop Earth from becoming such a mess. Nothing's worked. Now we're in its orbit, scrabbling around for resources on other planets, desperately trying to find ways to travel in large numbers a really long way away to another world before we run out of everything within reach.

I throw a load more vague questions at her, but she replies with a question of her own.

"Can you imagine now the stars in your dreams? How they moved?"

"Yes." That's better: I try less hard and what I want to say just pops up – no spoken words needed.

"Good."

"How is that good?" I was told on the last visit that what I had seen was the end of the universe. "That's bad, surely?"

"It means that you have a good pairing."

"Pairing?"

"Yes." There is a pause and then I'm aware of another set of voices. They talk in a language I can't understand before Rose-Anne talks to me directly.

"Come, Milo 8," she says. "I have consulted. I can confirm your pairing is nearly ready. Let's walk now."

I feel something solid under my feet. I look down and see a strip of blackness, stretching out into the distance like a path. The stars are still around me but they have slowed.

"Our journey is near its end."

"Journey? What journey?"

She ignores the question. I get a whiff of perfume; sweet roses with a hint of jasmine. How I imagined Rose-Anne's perfume to be. "I sound and soon will look like a person that you know. The same person that your pairing has seen. Our previous form was perhaps difficult for you." If she means the gloopy, green mess, yes; that was a little strange. Mind you; this whole experience is more than a little strange.

I still can't see her but I'm convinced now this is Rose-Anne, my 'non-girlfriend' from the compulsoral.

I ask an obvious question. "Am I in a compulsoral?"

"No. You are not."

"But you are in my compulsorals."

She pauses before replying: "Yes. We used them so we could check you were suitable."

"Suitable for what?"

Another pause. "Suitable for your pairing."

"I don't get it. What is a pairing?"

"You will discover that when you meet him. Then, we hope, you will be ready to do the right thing."

I desperately want to look at her, but still can't. I have to make do with her voice and smell. "Ready to do what right thing?"

"You will have a decision to make. You will find it difficult and you may decide one way and then the next. But, at the right time, you will know what is right. We hope."

Decide one way and the next? For someone who can't even decide what clothes I like, this sounds more than a little tricky.

"I don't think I will know." I say it with a confidence I haven't had since I was whisked away to wherever this is.

Why am I so confident? Well, for the first time in ages, I'm certain of one thing: I'm absolutely certain that I haven't the faintest idea what in Jupiter's name she's talking about.

Marcus

"Marcus... Marcus..."

"Stefan?"

"No, not Stefan."

Not Stefan. Of course, it's not Stefan. This is the girl who visited me in the hospital. I recognise the voice and that slightly awkward way of speaking. I open my eyes and I see her face, slightly blurred, peering over me. It is the face of the so-called doctor in the hospital.

"Are you well, Marcus?"

"Not really, no. Where am I?"

My head hurts and I feel a little dizzy. I blink a few times, trying to clear my eyes, then close them again. After a few moments, the dizziness lessens enough so I can risk opening them again. When I do, her face is still there, clearer, smiling down at me. I turn my head and try to look past her, but her head follows mine and she blocks my view.

"Wait for your eyes to adjust properly. Then you can look around."

For the moment, I decide that maybe I should be happy with just looking at her face. After all, it's a nice face to look at.

I blink a few more times and scratch my nose. Mum says

she can always tell when I am embarrassed about something because I always scratch my nose. I feel myself go red in the cheeks and, hoping she won't notice, try to cover it up by speaking again.

"I can see fine, now. I think I can sit up."

"No need. I will release the straps and you can float around."

"Float?"

"Yes. For now, you can float, but by the time we are out of the galaxy, it will feel normal again. Gravity will gradually adjust to your Earth's levels."

Out of the galaxy? Normal again? What is she talking about?

I feel a little release of pressure over my stomach and shoulders and her head disappears below me as I rise up. The view is replaced by... by... I have to shut my eyes as I suddenly feel very queasy.

"You will..." She pauses as she searches for the right words. "...get used to it. Open your eyes for a short while and then close them again. Repeat until you feel well."

I do as she suggests. Each time I open my eyes, I immediately want to shut them again; the vastness is too much to handle. Gradually, though, I keep them open for longer periods as my brain takes in the enormity of what is around me.

It's similar to the experience I had with this same girl

before in hospital, yet different. This is space: galaxies, stars... the universe, just as I saw from my hospital bed. Back then, I felt I was part of it. Now, I'm passing through it and, judging by the way the view keeps changing, I am doing it at an incredible speed. It's all around – top, bottom and sides – racing past me in a blur.

As an eight-year-old, watching reruns of the old TV programme Star Trek with Sean and sometimes Stefan when he came to stay over, I had imagined myself as an astronaut of the future, travelling the galaxy in a spaceship the size of a cruise liner. I was captain, of course, in charge of my own bridge full of people dressed in similar outfits to me, except mine was red to show I was the boss. I would be able to travel around the ship as I wished. Doors would open on my command, I could view planets we were about to land on in 3D glory by touching a sensor on my earlobe, and even order whatever food I liked which would then appear through a beam of light shining onto my tray. I would give a command and powerful laser guns would be fired from the ship by my first officer at the wave of her hand over the bridge's control panel, and the planet would be saved from marauding space baddies. When I was tired, I would retire to my simple, but comfortable quarters, and be rocked to sleep by the sounds of the sea and the smell of the salty breeze from my favourite beach on Earth.

It was all in my young head, but I imagined I was on a

solid spaceship, with walls, doors, corridors and real things around me as I watched the stars speed past the windows.

This isn't anything like that. I can see nothing solid at all, yet I can breathe and float around as if there were something around me.

"A spaceship made of glass," I say.

"Something you might call a spaceship, but no, not made of glass."

"Special plastic?"

"No."

She offers no more information about that, so I ask: "How big is it?"

"As big as you want it to be. It expands and contracts as we move around. Watch."

She kicks gently and passes right by me, continuing up and up until I can barely see the soles of her feet. It's like she has just gone off into space. I call out. "Wait!" and within moments she is back beside me.

"Did I cause you concern?" she asks.

"Well, yes!" This whole thing causes me concern! "Am I dreaming?"

"No. When you dream, it is bad for you. We sense that and we feel it is getting worse. That is how we know it is time."

I shut my eyes. The views around me are distracting and I need to think. I have so many questions that I don't know where to start.

I try to retrace my last steps on – and this sounds crazy to me, even as I think it – Earth. I was with Stefan. He went on ahead. I tried to catch him. No, I was trying to get a phone signal. Then I saw him on the path in some kind of green circle. After that? Well, after that, it's unclear. I blacked out. No! Not blacked out. I felt like it was the end of everything...

I suddenly feel myself sinking towards the deepest, most terrible place where nothing exists at all. The stars – the shoals of fish – have left. There's no light. No feeling. No nothing. It's horrible, but before I lose myself there, I'm yanked back, and her face is in front of me again.

"Do not," she says simply.

I'm struggling for breath, just like I did in the hospital many times, and just as I did when I was on the path with Stefan. This time it's anxiety.

"Breathe, and try to move those thoughts away. They are dangerous to you. You need to learn more control before you can deal with that place."

Between breaths, I manage to gasp, "How... do I... stop... them?"

"We have a solution, now that we know you are suitable."

"Suitable?"

"Suitable for your pairing."

"My what?"

"Suitable for your pairing. Then, we hope, you will be ready to do the right thing."

"What right thing?"

"You will have a decision to make. You will find it difficult and you may decide one way and then the next. But, at the right time, you will know what to do. We hope."

"I don't understand."

"Not yet, but you will."

Frustrated, I turn away. There they all are again; those stars – real stars – whizzing past.

"Does the ship have to be transparent? Can we block or change the view?"

I'm physically tired, but most of all I'm sick and tired of looking at stars.

"Yes. Choose what you would like to see. Think it."

My eight-year-old Star Trek Enterprise-like spaceship pops into my mind and, in an instant, I'm in a cabin – like the captain's cabin. There's a bed, a meal, and the sounds of the sea gently caressing my ears. The girl is sitting on a chair in the corner looking at me.

"I will go now. You need to rest." She gets up and the door opens. "Remember, Marcus: you have the power to direct your mind; what it does, what it feels, what it thinks."

I let out a sigh. "It was horrible seeing that nothing, seeing what was happening to the stars. That place was worse than any nightmare I've had."

She smiles at me as she turns to leave. "Marcus... if you make the right choice, your nightmares won't be nightmares anymore."

I try to take comfort from what she's said, but it was the word *'if'* that worries me the most.

Milo

None of the answers Rose-Anne gives me make any sense. It is so annoying!

I try to keep calm. "So, you hope I will make the right decision about something, but you won't tell me what that thing is?"

"Correct, Milo 8."

"What about when? Will you tell me when I need to make it?"

"You will make it at the right time."

That doesn't help at all. Not only do I not know what the decision is about, I don't even know when it will be. "How will I know I'm making the right decision about something if I don't know what or when it is?"

"You will know."

"You keep saying that!" I try a different approach. "How do you know I will make the right decision?"

"We do not know. We hope you will. We hope you will do it because you care."

"Doesn't everyone care?"

"No. Not everyone cares. You think life is important."

Suddenly, Rose-Anne is – her body is – right next to me. I can see the outline of her face, framed by the stars. She is exactly as I remember her from the compulsorals. She smiles and I can't help smiling back. It seems like we stay like that for ages, walking and smiling, walking and smiling.

Eventually, I feel a need to stop smiling and find out a bit more. If I can.

"Doesn't everyone think life is important?" I ask.

"No. Many want to live, but they don't value life. Not enough to really care about others. You do. And you have strength inside of you. You have the power and strength to make the right decision. You have control."

"Decision – what decision? And control over what?"

"You will have a decision to make. You will find it difficult and you may decide one way and then the next. But, at the right time, you will know what to do. We hope."

"I don't understand."

"Not yet, but you will." Suddenly, she stops. "We're nearly there."

I look around, surprised as nothing much has changed. The stars with the black path splitting them flow on and on, as far as I can see, into the distance.

"We're nearly where?"

"This is as far as we can go. We must leave you to meet your pairing. He comes from a different route because he is of a different time."

"Of a different time? None of this makes sense! Look, tell me: what is this pairing you keep going on about?"

"His name is Marcus."

"Marcus?"

"Yes." She smiles again and begins to fade away. "We don't know that you will survive. We hope you do."

"Survive... what, how...?"

"We thank you, and hope you will be successful."

I'm feeling confused and more than a little angry now. She speaks in riddles. "I don't know what you are talking about! Successful, how?"

Her voice is fading away too now. "You care. Remember that: you care."

And she's gone.

I look around, clueless as to what to do next.

What to do next is quickly decided for me when a sudden violent wave of sickness overwhelms me. I double over, moaning as my stomach threatens to explode. I break out into a hot sweat which, within seconds, turns into a violent shiver, starting from my knees and working itself up through my body like a tidal wave. Six or seven zaps to the back of my neck become one large, continuous thump, thump, thump, like a wayward freighter whacking the sides of the dock gates on landing. I don't know where to turn or how to make any of it go away. I screw my eyes shut tight and scream, willing this attack on my body to please, PLEASE! STOP!

Just when I think I can bear it no longer, something gives

way.

All that pain and sickness melts away and I'm left with a feeling of relief which quickly turns to happiness.

I'm happy because the stars have stopped moving and I finally see them for what they are. These are my stars – the ones I see in my nightmares – but they do not shoal like frightened fish. They stand proud and glorious, pulsing and shimmering their greetings to me. I am part of them and they are part of me.

I know now what she meant when Rose-Anne said that I care. I do care. I care about the stars, the universe, and every single living thing in it. It's a wonderful feeling, pure bliss.

Why then do I have this voice in my head telling me I should destroy them all?

Marcus

I wake with a start, on my back, staring up at a blue sky. The sounds of waves and distant squawking seagulls fill my ears, and I'd swear that's salt I can still smell. I turn my head and there's sea lapping against the shore projected on a wall in the same cabin where the girl had left me. Wearily, I swing my legs around and sit up. The girl has gone and so has the meal, which is a shame because I feel hungry.

"Enough seaside," I say to thin air, and the sounds and smells stop, a plain, light-blue wall replacing the scene.

I get up and walk stiffly towards the door which opens automatically, turn left into an empty corridor, and head for the Bridge. I know exactly where to go; after all, this is my ship that I've imagined and created. The lift takes me up at high speed right to the top, and I step out, expecting to see a hive of activity. But no one is there. The control panels and huge screen showing our journey through the galaxy are exactly as I imagined them to be (just like the Bridge on Star Trek's USS Enterprise). I walk around the perimeter of the Bridge, glancing at the smaller screens and listening to their bleeps and pings.

I do not notice the girl arrive so I jump slightly at her voice behind me.

"You slept well." No question, just a statement.

"I did." Like a baby, I realise. No hint of a bad dream.

"You notice we have what feels like your gravity."

I hadn't really. I knew I wasn't bobbing around any longer, but I was too distracted by the layout and workings of the ship to realise things felt normal from that point of view.

Ridiculously, I bend my knees and stamp my feet to prove that I'm attached to the floor. This results in a scratch of the nose when I realise that what I'm doing is just plain stupid and embarrassing. It occurs to me that Stefan would probably agree!

She laughs. It sounds a bit awkward, but it's nice. It makes me smile.

"The look of this ship is more comfortable for you," she says.

"Yes. I felt a bit sick without any walls."

"We are happy to provide whatever you need."

"Look..." I begin, but she interrupts me.

"I will explain what I can. Will you eat? You are hungry."

I sure am.

"Eat here or somewhere else?" she asks.

I take a look around the Bridge and then nod. "Well, it all seems to be under control here," I say briskly, trying to act like the famous Captain James T. Kirk. "Let's head to the dining quarters."

We say nothing on the way down the two levels to the eating hall, but I'm aware of her eyes on me. Embarrassed again, I try to keep my own fixed firmly ahead and my hands in my pockets to avoid scratching my nose.

When we arrive, there is a table already set out for us with two plates piled high with pieces of chicken, chips and peas. Glasses of frothy chocolate milkshake stand next to them. For a moment, I forget where I am as, head down, I tuck into the food. It's all delicious. Halfway through my fourth chicken thigh, I look up and realise that the girl hasn't touched hers.

"You have..." again that tiny pause as she tries to remember a word, "... ketchup on your chin."

Hastily, I run my sleeve across my mouth which makes her smile, then take a glug of the milkshake, being careful to use the straw provided to avoid further mess.

"I am interested in you humans and your need to eat different types of energy. You must explain it to me sometime. For now, though, ask me questions, if you so wish."

I lean back in the chair and puff out my cheeks. Where to start? I keep it simple. "What is your name?"

"We do not need names, yet I understand that you do, so call me Rose-Anne."

"Rose-Anne?"

"Yes."

"You said, 'we'; who is 'we'?"

"That is complicated. We are a collection of two people. I am a mixture of both of them."

"I don't understand."

"I agree; you do not."

That line of questioning seems to be blocked off, so I try another route. "Where are we going?"

"On a journey. You might describe it as going to the edge of your experience."

I decide that, as much as I understand the words 'experience' and 'the edge of', it's too much for my little brain to take in when they are used together, so I just repeat what she said. "To the edge of my experience?"

"Yes."

She offers nothing more, so I ask: "Like the edge of the universe?"

"If that helps you to understand, then, yes. Your friend was right when he told you that you are important. You are very important."

"Stefan!" I feel a sudden surge of panic. "Where is he? Is he alright?"

"Yes, he is well. He has completed his role."

"His role? His role in what?"

"To guide you back to the lake at the right time. Without him, you might not have come... willingly. It needed to be your choice." I don't remember being that willing to go there. Still... "He helped you make that choice. He will remember nothing of this."

I have a sudden vision of him upside down in the green circle. She seems to react to my thought by continuing: "It was necessary to place him in the circle so that he does not remember. He is not needed any longer. If you decide otherwise, that is your choice."

"You talk about my choice. I didn't choose to be here. You brought me."

"Yes. But now the choices are yours. You have a bigger choice to make very soon. That will be your choice alone."

"What bigger choice?"

"You will know when it is time."

I shrug and hold my hands out, hoping she will go on to explain more. She doesn't. Instead, she repeats herself: "You will know when it is time."

This might not be an important question to ask next, but something is bothering me. "Was that your spaceship we saw at the lake?"

"It was necessary for you to believe it was part of it."

"Necessary for me to believe? What do…"

She doesn't allow me to finish the question. "It has now become as one with this." She waves a hand around, indicating the ship, I assume, as she says this.

"You didn't arrive on Earth in it, then?"

"It was there to attract you and your friend to the lake. It did that."

"Did you mean for us to fall off the cliff?"

"That was your choice to be up there. It seems now it was part of the necessary journey so that you can be ready at the right time."

"You keep mentioning the right time. The right time for what?"

"You have to arrive at the edge of your experience at exactly the right time."

I'm still confused. "You said something like, 'When you dream, it is bad and it's getting worse.' That's how you knew it was time?"

"Yes. When we came to you in the hospital, we showed you your power. You saw the stars leaving and said it was going to happen soon. Then, you dreamed badly, with no control. Now you are nearly ready to control your mind and dreams and, we hope, make the right decision. You will control what happens next. You have the power to control the destiny of the human race."

I put my hands over my face. Up until that point, I was, as hard as it is to believe, prepared to go along with what she was saying. But when she says that I will control the destiny of the human race, it's too much.

I stand up and accidentally knock her milkshake over. It shows what a state of shock I'm in when I barely blink as the brown sticky liquid, which was about to slop onto the floor, drips and disappears.

I hold my head in my hands. "Argghh... what are you talking about with all this power and control? It's nonsense. I'm only a boy. What can I do?"

"You can do a lot. The stars you see are important. Control them and you control your race's destiny."

Now she's talking about controlling stars. This is madness! I feel an urge to stomp around and wave my arms in the air, so I do exactly that. She stays seated, watching my tantrum with interest. After a minute of this, I'm exhausted and, with nothing else to do, and no real other place to go, I sit back down opposite her... And scratch my nose.

We sit in silence for a short while, with me staring at her plate of food and she, no doubt, staring at me. Eventually, I mutter, somewhat wearily, "You mentioned that I should control the stars. No one can control the stars."

"You can."

"How?"

"You will know when you know."

"Know when I will know? How will I know when I know?"

"Just that: you will know."

I gather up enough energy for another stomp around, and this time I don't stop. Luckily, the door out of the dining area opens automatically. Otherwise, I would've crashed right through it.

Shoal

Milo

I've been left alone amongst the stars. Alone, lost and clueless. What am I expected to do now?

The good news is that the terrible throbbing pain I felt before has not come back... so far.

I've taken the pain as some sort of warning about me making the wrong decision when the time comes. Whether it has come from Rose-Anne and her band of... of whatever they are, or whether it comes from something deep inside of me, I just don't know. If it is a warning, I see what I'm being warned against. That feeling of wanting to destroy everything came out of the blue. One second, I was enjoying my stars, the next, I wanted to blow them up. How I would even do that – let alone why – I really don't know.

I figure that I have two possible choices from here. One: continue along the black path in the direction I am facing, or two: turn back. I look both ways and quickly realise that I only have one choice really, and that is to carry on.

So, I walk.

As I walk, I start to feel something I have never felt before. I begin to feel stronger, more powerful, like I have some tremendous force within me. It seems that I have been given a gift, and it's a gift to decide on the fate of the stars, possibly the whole universe. How cool is that? It gives me a surge of energy, and I stride along with a feeling of purpose.

I don't need to worry about where the path's going; someone with my power does not concern themselves with little things like that. I am just here, walking, striding, doing as I wish. I don't need to follow anything. Everything will follow what I do!

I quicken the pace, not because I'm in a hurry, but for no other reason than that it feels good and it's my choice. I break into a jog, then a run and before I know it, I am sprinting as fast as I can. I know my lungs are working overtime, yet I barely notice it. I am power and energy, strength and might. A god, almost...

With that last thought, I come to a sudden halt. A god, almost? No! Not almost a god; I am a god. Is that possible? Rose-Anne said I had an important decision to make; that I had control. If I have the power to decide over the stars then, yes, I must be a god. Gods ruled the heavens and that is exactly what I am doing. The heavens are under my control. I am their judge and jury. I will choose what – if anything – happens to them.

Rose-Anne said something else. She told me that I care about life. That's true – I do. But that's because it is mine to care about. All of it – people, life, planets, stars, the whole thing is mine to care about. Mine to care about, mine to control, mine to decide what happens to it.

You better watch out, Universe:

Milo 8 has the power… and he is coming for you!

Marcus

I stomp around the corridors of the ship for I don't how long, not knowing where I am heading, my mind spinning round and round like a demented washing machine.

Rose-Anne had been clear; she said that I had to control the stars. But in my nightmares, they are running away. I wonder if, somehow, part of me is making them run away, destroying them. But how can that be true? And is it really possible that I can control the stars?

Eventually, I come to a dead-end and look up to realise that I am at the doors to the lift which will take me up and onto the bridge. I go in and, when they open again, I am faced once more with that same, familiar, circular control room I had seen so many times in films – the Bridge of the USS Enterprise.

I look around; it is still empty.

I walk down the steps and slump onto the black swivel chair that is normally taken by my hero, Captain James T. Kirk. As I run my hand along the armrests, I toy with the idea of pressing some of the buttons on them to see what would happen. There is nothing to stop me, so I do exactly that. I wait for a few seconds but everything stays the same, including the familiar big screen in front of me which has stars rushing past. Rose-Anne had said the ship was there to make me feel more comfortable. But like the chair I am sitting on, the stars on the screen feel like a fake. It's all a fake. I feel like a fake.

I let out a sigh and, with my elbow resting on the arm, put my hand over my face and hold it over my eyes and forehead. The washing cycle that is my brain has at least slowed to that last part after the final spin where it just goes around once or twice more while it's waiting for someone to open the door and take the clothes out.

It should give me some relief but, instead, it just feels like my brain is left a soggy, tangled mess. I could do with help.

"Help." The voice is quiet. I barely hear it. "Help, please."

I look up and around me, but the Bridge is still empty. I walk over to the doors behind and they open as I approach. The lift that had taken me up is still there, but that too is empty.

"Help."

There it is again. The voice is barely audible, but it does not sound particularly worried. There is no real urgency in it. It sounds more like a simple request rather than a desperate cry for help.

I realise also, as I hear it again, that it sounds awfully familiar.

"Stefan? Is that you? Where are you?"

I walk around the outside of the Bridge on the upper

deck, checking the screens as I go. They make no real sense to me at all; just flashing lights on one, what looks like sound waves on a couple of them, and nothing but numbers and symbols on others.

"Help."

"Stefan?"

I finally track in on its source and realise the voice is coming from the main screen, dead centre. I return to the captain's chair and stand in front of it to get the best view. Right in that centre point, I can make out a star that, unlike the other ones, is not moving. I soon work out that it is not a star at all, as Stefan's face comes into view. It's his face and ginger hair, rotating slowly as it gets bigger and bigger. The cry for help becomes more desperate sounding, the bigger and closer the face gets to me.

"Help! Help!"

In a panic, I look around for — for what? I don't know. I shout out to Rose-Anne, but I sense she is nowhere nearby. Stefan's pleas turn to a scream, so loud that I have to block my ears.

Just as his face takes up nearly the whole screen it comes to a stop, resting awkwardly in an upside-down position. I think back to when I last saw him at the lake, inside the green ring. He was upside down then and Rose-Anne said he would be returned to his hospital bed, his recent memory wiped for his own protection. Why is he here now, then?

There is another scream from Stefan – more of a yelp, really – and it is at that moment that it sinks in why he is here. It's because I've asked for him. I need him here to help me. I can't do any of this without him. As annoying as he can be on occasions, Stefan is my rock, the person who keeps my feet firmly on the ground.

He has always been there for me since we were young kids. If there's something I need at the moment as I hurtle through space faster than anything I could imagine (in a spaceship that has been built out of my head because the "real" one is so complicated and advanced that it doesn't need basic things such as engines, fuel or even walls) then that something is my best friend who might help me make some sense of all this.

I can't do this without Stefan.

Instinctively, I wave my hand, the screen goes blank, and then I hear a gasp behind me. I turn around and then can't help but burst into laughter. Stefan is on the captain's chair, but his head is on the seat, his legs pedalling away furiously above him.

"Help!" he says again and then stops. He pulls his eyebrows up (or rather down, bearing in mind he is upside down) into that exaggerated position he puts them into when I've said or done something stupid.

I cock my head to one side, smile and then say the coolest thing I've ever said: "Ah, Mr Bond... I've been expecting you," before grabbing his legs and helping him down.

Stefan's hungrier than I was earlier when I ate with Rose-Anne. We're back in the dining room and he is tucking into his third bean burger and second lot of fries, washed down with a bucket load of chocolate milkshake. It passes through my mind, briefly, how an alien "ship" knows how to make all this stuff. Surprisingly, he doesn't seem as shocked as I felt when I first arrived on this vessel, but then again, he always has been led by what his stomach tells him to do. Right now, it appears to be telling Stefan to fill it up with junk food.

He wipes away some tomato sauce from his mouth with the back of his hand, takes another glug of shake and then leans back in his chair, giving me that look he gives me now and again that says, 'Well, are you going to tell me what's going on, or not?'

"I thought you might be more put out than you seem," I say. "Aren't you shocked to be here?"

He takes a slow casual look around before settling his gaze back on me. This is what I mean about him being annoying sometimes. I think I'm cool because I've come up with the James Bond saying. He is always cool, even when he should be at least a tiny bit surprised to be here.

"Well, yes, I guess so. But don't forget, I have already been put upside in a green ring before you went off without me by the lake. Also, it wasn't me that didn't want to believe aliens had landed."

"But you're on the Starship Enterprise."

"True. But if aliens are involved – and I have no doubt now that they are – I would expect them to do something a bit unusual. I admit, I hadn't necessarily expected to be on Captain Kirk's ship, but I'm sure you can tell me a little bit more about that."

See what I mean about being annoying? And cooler than me? I try to gain the upper hand by saying, "I brought you here."

"Obvs."

"Yes, well, I decided that I needed help. They wanted to wipe your memory, but I've... I've overruled them. I want you here."

"I knew you'd need me." He grins. "That was quite a ride, though, especially the last part towards the end. You know that rollercoaster I nearly refused to go on at Southend?"

"The one I bet you two weeks' pocket money you wouldn't do?" (Also, the one I lost two weeks' pocket money on – he's stubborn as well as cool). "Where you screamed the whole way round on?" (Not always cool).

"Yeah. It was like that. I didn't mind the spinning, but as soon as I could feel I was going up, I knew there would be a down part. That's when I started really calling for help. I might be the handsomest, cleverest and smoothest person ever, but put me on a rollercoaster and I'm like a big baby. Can I get a yoghurt? One of those vanilla ones with sprinkles in triangle pots?"

"I expect so. Look... as I say, I need your help. They want me to control the stars."

"So that you can save the world, as we already knew. So?"

"So... so..." I'm feeling impatient now. "It's a big responsibility."

"Yes." His yoghurt has now appeared, and he sighs as he takes his first spoonful. "Yum."

"I just thought I should have someone with me that I can bounce ideas off."

"I'm honoured." He has already finished the pot and is now licking the inside of the foil lid.

"Put that down, will you?" My voice is sharp and he does as I ask, with, I'm pleased to say, a trace of guilt – and yoghurt – on his face.

"So, tell me how." He leans back and folds his arms. This is his "listening" position. At least he appears to be trying to take it seriously now.

"I don't know, really."

I tell him about what has happened since I last saw him. I tell him about Rose-Anne and what she and they are expecting me to do. How it will all be down to me to make some sort of big decision on controlling the stars. When I finish, I notice that, while I was talking, he had scrunched up the foil lid into a ball. The pot is on its side and he starts to absentmindedly nudge the ball towards it with his finger.

"Well?" I say. "What do you think?"

He pushes the chair back and lowers his head until it's level with the table, then lines up his eyes so that they're directly behind his ball which he has placed on the edge. He puts a finger on his thumb and prepares to flick it into the pot.

"I think," he says adjusting his fingers for the shot, "we need to talk to this Rose-Anne again. She's our number one target..." He lets loose and the silver ball goes sailing wide and way over the top. "... and that line would have been way better if I'd got the ball into the pot. Though I'm quite happy where it ended up."

I take the silver ball out of my hair and throw it back at him, pleasingly hitting him squarely on the nose. "Well, I've not seen her for a bit, so that might be harder to do than you think, but I'm fed up watching you play with your food. Come on. Let's go see if we can find ourselves an alien."

And I know that last sentence would have sounded so much cooler if Stefan had said it.

Milo

I'm still thinking, trying to come to terms with my new-found role as a god.

I decide that, although it might be quite fun having a lot of power, it doesn't make whatever I have to do that easy. There's lots to consider, lots of things to weigh up before decisions are taken. And it looks like there might be some important decisions coming up soon, so I better be prepared.

I go back to that line of Rose-Anne's: "Not everyone cares." Perhaps some of the people I have known are not so good. Perhaps there are things around that are not so good. Perhaps, then, it's my responsibility to decide who – or what – is good and who, or what, should be saved. That could be a tough one, but maybe I need to just suck it up and get on with it.

The responsibility is mine.

Mine.

No one else's, not Rose-Anne or anybody else's... just mine.

If they're giving me all this power then it's down to me to use it the way I see fit.

Rose-Anne wanted me to choose life, but she is not in

charge of the heavens – I am. I will decide what to do with the good ones and the bad ones. I have that power. Not her. I feel angry at her for thinking she can control what I do. She has no right. Nor have all the other people who have let me down in my life.

The other people...

My nursery mother barely had any time for me. She only started to pretend she was interested when she realised that I could earn good credits flying freighters around. The more success for the clones she looks after, the more credits for her. She doesn't actually care about me as a person. She has left me to live on my own and make my way the best I could. She has never shown me any love, so why should I care about her?

Then there are the people who use me to pilot their stupid freighters. They don't care either. They just use me. I'm the youngest and best pilot they have, but what do they care? No one cares.

All those people who ignored me in the eaters, on the walkways, and even at the leisure bowl where I go to play sports, all think they're better than me. Think they can control me.

The people who make the compulsorals ... how could a god like me ever fall for what they did? They tried to run my life, choose what I ate, drank, wore, where I went.

As for Rose-Anne and her alien 'friends' – what right do

they have to do what they have done? Who do they think they are, picking me up in their fancy spaceship and choosing where to take me?

There will be no more of this.

No more.

NO MORE!

I feel rage boiling up inside of me. And I find that I like it. It shows how powerful I truly am. These people who want to control my life are nothing. I am the powerful one. I am the one who will decide what happens next, what happens to them and to everything else. I am the one in control.

I can control the stars.

I feel like I am growing. My body, my mind, the energy thrusting through every pore, every cell inside of me. If I want to throw thunderbolts, like Thor, I can. He is a tiny god compared to me. I am much stronger than him. Much more powerful than him. After all, I have the power to decide whether the stars live or die. My stars will go where I tell them, do what I tell them. And there is nothing – and no one – to stop me.

Especially not a pairing called Marcus.

Marcus

We check at the Bridge first, just in case Rose-Anne has gone there.

Stefan can't resist pressing one of the buttons on the chair and saying, "Attention. This is First Officer Stefan Kaprinsky here. Lieutenant Rose-Anne report to the Bridge, immediately."

"How do you know that's the right button?" I ask.

"I don't, but it's worth a go. Hang on... I'll change the message." He presses the button again. "Ignore that last order. Ahem... Lieutenant Rose-Anne report to the Bridge if you're there and this button works. If this button doesn't work, ignore that order. If it does work and we're not here, come and find us." He pauses while he thinks. "Ahem... over and out."

"You can be such a numpty sometimes."

"At least I'm doing something."

He's right; that's why I've called for him to be here, so he can come up with ideas.

"I'm sorry, Stefan. What do you think we should do?"

"I reckon her not being here is some sort of test, like a problem to be solved."

"Go on."

"Right, let's think. Where does Captain Kirk go when there's a problem?"

"Why? This ship and the Bridge aren't real, you know. It's all been invented so I don't feel sick travelling in a glass spaceship."

"Okay. Change it then."

"What to?"

"A place where you can normally find things. This ship is too big. Unless she does come to us, we'll never find her."

And then it hits me. If she wanted us to find her, she'd be here now. Or, rather, if I wanted to find her, I would be able to. I realise that I don't need her. This is something for me to sort out... with Stefan's help.

I say as much.

"That figures," he says. He speaks into the intercom again. "Forget the last two announcements, Lieutenant Rose-Anne. We have the situation under control. Out."

"Will you please start taking this more seriously?"

"Okay. Serious face..." He furrows his eyebrows and purses his lips. He just looks like he's in pain now, but I appreciate the effort.

"Rose-Anne said that we are heading for the edge of my experience. I took that to mean the edge of the universe, if there is such a thing, because all the stars are leaving and they have to go somewhere."

"That's weird, but carry on."

"She also said that I had the power to control my mind now. That's why you're here and why the ship looks like this. But where we are heading exactly — can I control that? Do I want to? Where else would I go?"

A thought strikes me: home is where I want to go, but I know that's not possible. Not yet, anyway. Or not exactly in the way that I might like to.

Another thought nudges away at the back of my brain. "You said something important earlier on, Stefan. What was it?"

"I'm always saying important things."

I roll my eyes. "This was something really important. What was it?" I snap my fingers. "Got it! You said the ship was too big."

"It is. I said you should change it. Change it to a place where we can find things. But that was when we were looking for Rose-Anne. Apparently, we're not anymore. I don't know what we're looking for now."

"Nor do I, but I do know that, when we arrive at the edge of the universe, or wherever it is we're going, I need to be ready. I need to have everything in place around me so that, if I do work it out, I can deal with it quickly."

As I speak, the Bridge begins to shimmer and then fade away. Gone are the walls, the screen, the chair, the bleeps. The ship goes back to its normal form and we are briefly laid wide open to the black of space, just as I experienced earlier with Rose-Anne.

But it doesn't stay like that for long. Soon, more walls appear around us; signs on walls I can't yet make out, furniture, a window, and a door… my bedroom door with my dressing gown hanging up on it. These are posters on the wall, not signs, I realise. My posters. Plain walls with posters that have replaced my old Spiderman wallpaper.

Lines waver to the left of the door and then settle down to form my shelves with books and the dying Yucca plant that I keep forgetting to water. The curtains close and a bedside light switches on. Suddenly, I'm at my desk sitting on my swivel chair – not as swish as Captain Kirk's – but it still feels good. I turn round and Stefan is sitting on the duvet on my bed. The cover is red and white and has David Beckham and some of the other Manchester United legends standing up holding a cup. It's an old duvet set that Sean got for me from somewhere. I've had it since I started getting into football when I was seven. It's a bit faded now, but I can't bear to part with it.

"So, this is the place where you can find everything, is it?" Stefan asks.

"Mostly, yes, I guess."

"In this mess?"

"It's tidier than usual. There's hardly anything on the floor."

"Call this tidy?" He puts his foot under a sock and flicks it towards me. I let it land harmlessly on the desk next to me.

It is indeed much tidier than usual, which is partly why I know that this isn't my actual bedroom. It doesn't feel quite right. But it's a place – a room – in my mind where I can find things. In my real bedroom, if I lose a book, a pen, my watch or phone, it will always be in here, despite the mess and despite what I tell Mum. I always huff and puff around the house searching, before eventually admitting that, all along, it was under my bed or tucked away on my shelves somewhere.

"Right," I say decisively to Stefan. "You check under the bed. Take everything out. I'll go through the shelves."

"What are we looking for?"

I shrug and then stand on my chair to get to a better height to get to the shelves.

"Let me get this right: you want me to look under your bed for something, but you don't know what it is yet?"

I grab the first folder I see and flick through the pages. It's a geography folder, an Easter holiday project I did when I was ten. "Yes. Just do it, Stefan."

Suddenly I feel like there isn't much time left. Perhaps the spaceship is close to its destination.

"You're not going to give me a clue, then?"

"If I could, I would. Just look."

"O...kay."

He slumps off the bed and starts to pull out the boxes

and other things I keep underneath it. I ignore the "bleurgh" sound he makes as I realise that he's probably found another of my smelly sports socks. I continue to go through the files and books, skimming through the pages before picking up the next one. As I do so, I try to keep my mind open, a hint of the control that Rose-Anne taught me. I keep it open, yet focussed. Focussed on... focussed on... and then it's suddenly there, right in front of me.

A picture. A picture I drew when I was six years old, drawn on a piece of A4 with multiple lines where it's been folded and then unfolded. It's just there, at the back of a Pokémon annual I was given for Christmas in that same year.

I take it out and carefully step down from the chair.

"You can stop looking," I say to Stefan's feet which are surrounded by all the stuff that he has pulled out. "I've got it."

There is a muffled reply and then Stefan worms his way out from underneath my bed.

"That's disgusting under there," he says. He stands up and wipes his hands on his trousers. "There was a pizza box right at the back. I didn't open it."

"Look," I say.

He takes the picture from me. "You're no better at drawing now, are you? Who's that supposed to be?"

"That's me. Look closely."

"Your hair is a different colour. Did they only have red and blue felt tips at wherever you did this?"

"I did it at school. Don't you remember? We had a man come in to talk to us about space for the day."

"I do remember that now you say it! The guy was a bit geeky – a bit like you – but he made it lots of fun. Loads of different activities. We built a space station out of cardboard boxes and plastic bottles."

"Exactly. At the end, we had to draw a picture of what we thought space was like. Most the kids drew space rockets and meteors flying about everywhere. I drew this. Look closely at what's behind me."

Stefan pulls it closer to his face. "Squiggles."

"No, not squiggles. Look again."

"Is it a map of some sort?"

"I reckon."

"A map to where?"

"A map to where I hope I'll find some answers."

"Huh?"

"A map to..." And then he's gone. And Rose-Anne is next to me. We're standing at a gate, surrounded by stars. My stars, the ones I see in my nightmares.

"We are nearly there," she says. "You are ready now."

"Am I?" I look around nervously.

She smiles an encouraging smile that does nothing whatsoever to encourage me, then points to the map.

I glance down at it. She tells me that I'm ready. Is this map meant to prove I am, to show me where to go?

Surely, a map is only useful if you know your destination?

Part 3 – To the Centre

Milo

There's no danger of me calming down anytime soon. If anything, I am getting more and more angry as I stomp onwards. This path goes on forever! When I get to the end of it, I'll need to release this anger before I explode. In fact, that is exactly what I will do – explode! That's how I'll do it. That's how I'll make those stars run away from me. They won't stand a chance. I am the shark and they are the tiny, tiny fish, too scared to meet me head-on. They will gather together and then run away as quickly as they can; a shoal, too frightened to stick around.

I curl up my fingers in my right hand, bunching them into a fist, like Thor's hammer ready to unleash its power and wrath. I'll be Thor, but on a grand scale... just as soon as I can get to the end of this path!

As soon as I think that, I start to tire and slow down. The anger is still there, but I need a few minutes to gather my thoughts, make my plans for attack. I think I can see the end of the path, not far away.

I slow to a snail's pace. My breathing has been quick and

deep and my chest is telling me now to slow that right down too, to suck in as much air as it can so I can recover.

My fist is still in a ball, but some of the urgency has gone out of me. That's a good thing, I decide. I can't be hasty. Gods need to be thoughtful as well as strong. Yes, I have enough power to do what I like, but power has to be used properly if I am to succeed.

I see what appears to be a gate in front of me. It looks like one of those huge wooden gates you might see in the middle of the wall in the grounds of a castle. Rounded at the top, it has long vertical slats of wood, huge black metal hinges, and a rusty circular handle on the righthand side. I'm so surprised to see it that it stops me in my tracks. I blink and then it's directly in front of me, almost right up against my face. I take a couple of steps back. There's a small piece of paper pinned to the centre. On it is written my name in bright red letters.

I remove the pin, take the paper down, and the gate disappears. I should be surprised at something disappearing like that, but after what I've been through nothing surprises me.

I examine the paper which has been folded over many times. I remember this piece of paper and I remember writing my name and folding it like that.

When I was eight, someone told me that, no matter how big a piece of paper was, it could only be folded a maximum of seven times. Real paper was hard to come by, but I was determined to prove I could do it more than seven times. I didn't realise that you needed a much bigger piece of paper than the piece I had to even stand a chance, but I was determined to try. I managed four with the small piece I had. Incredibly, this is that same piece of paper, a piece of paper that I had thrown in the waste chute long ago.

I unfurl it and look at the drawing I did as an eight-year-old boy. It was a picture of me in space, probably the only drawing I have ever done on real, actual paper. Behind it, I've drawn a load of squiggles. I look more closely at them. No, they're not squiggles. This is a map.

Now, I no longer feel anger at all. It is time to be sensible, calm and, most importantly, ready. Ready because I sense that the pairing the voices told me about – Marcus – is coming soon. I'm certain that he is trouble. A danger, here to stop me, to control me, to do something that everyone else tries to do. I can't let him do that. I'm the one that calls the shots here.

I have my map and now I'm ready to head into the stars. I'll have a good look around, then I'll decide what to do with them.

Shoal

Marcus

I look at the map again then, still clueless, stare at the gate in front of us. It's wooden and very old, just like the one Stefan and I once dared each other to go through when we got lost in the grounds of Woburn Abbey.

"Go," Rose-Anne says.

I shrug, and then reach for the handle, but the gate disappears before I touch it. Still in front of me are the stars. Billions and billions and billions of them. I'm not sure I can face them.

I think of Stefan. What would he say in this situation? What would he do?

He'd tell me to get on with it. He was the one who led us to the lake and the spacecraft in the first place. He was the one who dared to get a closer look up on the cliff, dared to return there to find out what had happened to the spacecraft. Dared to explore. Dared to go through the gate first at Woburn Abbey. Yes, Stefan would tell me to face it and deal with it.

Still, I have my doubts.

"Where do I go?"

"Why ask me, Marcus? You know."

"Do I?"

"Yes."

"How will I know when I have arrived?"

Her answer is predictable: "You will know. Remember that you're in control now."

"What do I do when I get there?"

"You will know that too. You will make the right decision, Marcus. When the time comes."

"How do I even get there?"

"You move. Like we showed you."

"You mean..." And then I remember that amazing experience I had in my hospital bed when Rose-Anne visited. That feeling of movement, of being part of the universe, happiness like I could never imagine before the nothingness became my nightmare.

I look at her. "I don't understand." She opens her mouth, about to speak, but I interrupt, suddenly annoyed. "And don't say, 'I will know.' That's not good enough. I need more from you." She raises an eyebrow but says nothing. I don't want to get angry, but it's so frustrating. "You come to my home, my planet, pluck me from it and then take me on a wild journey across the universe in a crazy spaceship. You take me away from my best friend, then bring him back and then take him away again. You put me in my bedroom, lead me to a map, and now you say I will know what to do." Her mouth opens again, but I'm on a roll now as my anger mounts. "And I know what you are going to say. You're going to tell me that I'm controlling it. That I have the power to control it. That I will know what to do..." I make my voice higher, a very bad attempt to mimic her. "... when the time comes."

On another occasion, I could imagine Stefan and I laughing about that very bad impression, but not this time. Rose-Anne's face remains still. Apart from the eyebrow which has gone back down, she has kept the same expression. I stop my rant and my eyes drop in embarrassment.

When I look down, I see a light that extends out as far as I can see to my left towards the stars. The map I found in my so-called bedroom is still in my hand, the light coming directly from it. Like on a Sat Nav, the route is laid out, a clear route to get to where I need to go. Except, I can't see the endpoint. I have no doubt, though, that this is the start and the direction I must head in.

"Are you coming with me?" I ask.

"Is that your wish?" I nod. "It is not possible. I have come further than I did for your pairing."

"My pairing?"

"His name is Milo."

"What... who...Milo, did you say?" But I'm talking to nothing because she is gone.

And it's shortly after that when things start to go badly wrong.

Milo

The problem with maps is that they are only really useful if you have an idea of where you are trying to get to. Somewhere from the back of my mind a lesson about stellar maps, when I was plugged into one of the learning downloads, pops into the front of my brain.

To learn how to navigate the stars, the lesson started with 3D pictures of the old Earth which changed to 2D pictures of what that looked like. Flat and confusing is what it looked like, if you ask me!

Before they had guidance systems, people used to use these flat pictures to help them plan how to move from one place to another. They would put their finger on the place they started at, use a finger from the other hand to point at where they wanted to go, and then move the first finger along things they called roads until they got there, deciding whether they had to go left, right or straight on when other roads joined the ones they were on. Crazy, right? But we had to start with these to understand how the more complicated star maps worked.

It must have affected me because I drew the map that I am now holding in my hands. I've done a 2D version of the stars, with lines showing routes, or roads through them.

There is nothing to say where to finish or what's at the end of it. Still, it's all I've got and I had better work it out quickly; my pairing, something tells me, is close. I feel like that could be bad news.

A light appears, coming from the map. It looks like it's pointing the way, so I set off. I move slowly, to begin with, not walking but kind of floating. I can feel, almost, that I'm on the map and heading in the right direction. The lines I have drawn are clear pathways, and I'm on those pathways now as I move from one star to the next. The universe opens up to me and I get quicker, more confident in my movements, more confident in my ability. I fly, spin and swoop from one place to another, using galaxies and other stars as markers, signposts, to find my way around. Yet, somehow, they are all familiar. I feel they are almost part of me and I part of them.

The stars seem to nod as I go past, a sign of respect as if they understand the power I have and what I might decide to do. They must know that their future is in my hands. That is a decision for when I get there (wherever *there* is) but, for now, I enjoy the ride, safe in the knowledge that I am in control...

...until, suddenly, I realise that I no longer am.

Marcus

I set off.

It starts okay, as I travel from point to point, star to star, galaxy to galaxy. But soon, any feeling of control I thought I had, disappears. I can see the pathways around me, the ones I drew on my map from star to star, but I can't stay on them. I am a long way away from the magical feeling I had in the hospital when I felt I was part of the universe.

It's almost as if the universe is pushing me around, trying to hurt me. No sooner do I see one of my lines on the map and head for the next star or galaxy, than I am pushed off course and I have to scrabble like mad to get back on it again. I feel like I'm the metal ball in a pinball machine, pinging off each star, struggling to avoid the black hole that is between the levers at the bottom.

I fly, spin and swoop from one place to another, none of it pleasant, none of it controlled now. Each time I get near a star, it attacks me. At least, it seems that way with them spurting out massive balls of fire. I have to duck and dive my way around. Why are they trying to hurt me?

Somehow, I manage to claw myself back to stay roughly on the route on the map, but I am beginning to get tired and wonder whether I can keep this up. After one particularly violent rejection by a galaxy, I begin to take it personally. How would they like being pushed around like this?

I start to feel something I have not had for a long while, not since I was a young kid when Stefan went off on my bike one day without telling me.

I feel really, really angry.

And suddenly the stars begin to back off. Each time I go near, they move away. I find it funny and can't help laughing at them. If Stefan were here with me, he would find this funny too, I'm sure. The stars shrink away. Scared by my anger, they seem no longer able to push me away. I am pushing them instead. They shimmer, wobble, fade, lose strength. They think they will be safe in bigger numbers. I'll teach them. I'll show them who is in charge, who is in control.

I laugh louder.

And the stars and the galaxies gather together, scared.

Very soon, they begin to shoal, just like fish.

Milo

I am standing on a silver disc; I know I have arrived. My map has taken me from the very edge, right to this point. I look around at the beauty that is everywhere. The colours, the shapes, the life on distant planets. How could I ever think of destroying it?

All the anger I felt before and during part of my journey here has disappeared, drained away from me. Because I'm here to protect it, not destroy it. Everything I have done has led me to this moment. I will do anything to keep what is around me. It is so beautiful.

But then it changes. Some of the stars and galaxies are moving towards each other. They start to assemble into thousands of huge separate clumps; sausage-like, then thinner, then rounder – kidney-shaped – transforming every second. One cluster seems to almost float past my nose. Others are more distant, snaking along at first but then starting to build up speed, twisting and turning in different directions. I have seen this before, of course: they are huddling together in fear, like great shoals of fish.

Spooked by something, they panic, and start to break up into smaller shoals. They rush past, bright different colour specks of light, all heading in the same direction. Massive long streams of them. Away, away, away from me. Away to the other end of the universe, towards nothing. Away towards the end of everything.

I try to call to them, to reassure them. They don't need to be scared of me. I try to tell them that it will be okay.

But it won't be okay as I realise that I am in the middle of my nightmare.

The time has come.

The stars are leaving.

It's then that I realise why they are so scared. Someone is making them scared.

He is making them leave.

There he is.

I see him now: Marcus, my pairing.

Marcus

There he is.

I see him now: Milo, my pairing.

I ignore the stars for the moment – they can wait – and I float towards the figure standing on a silver disc. I was expecting someone more powerful looking, but he is tiny, not important looking at all, just a kid.

He has no right to stand there – that spot is where I should be. I am stronger, wiser. I am in control here, and if he doesn't like what I'm doing, well... he will soon find out how powerful I am.

I have made my decision. The shoals of stars are there to do what I want them to. They tried to hurt me; it's time to teach them a lesson. I'm sending them away, for good.

My pairing is either with me or against me.

Gracefully, I land on my feet at one end of the disc, about ten meters away from him. I can see his face now, framed by a mop of straggly hair with a fringe that partly covers his face. His hair's weird; blue with white on the top, wavy and maybe a little longer and thicker than mine. He is also dressed strangely, all in white: white ankle-high boots, white what looks like jogging bottoms, weird white kneepads and a plain white vest with off-white stripes down the side. His dress sense is dreadful! He even wears his bracelets on his upper arms rather than his wrists. I don't usually care what other people wear – I am hardly a fashion model myself – but he does look ridiculous. Just looking at him makes me feel like it wouldn't matter if he was on my side or not. He's not someone I would want to hang around with – too embarrassing!

I puff my chest out – my new-found power has gone to my head! – and I start to stride towards him. As I do so, he flicks his head back and his stupid hair bounces up for a second. It stops me in my tracks. It's then that I realise that, apart from his clothes and hair, he is the spitting image…

Milo

… He is the spitting image of me, apart from his clothes and hair. I think I can even make out a small birthmark under his eye, a bit like mine, except his is on the opposite cheek.

He walks towards me, dressed like someone out of one of the history learning blocks I studied when I was a young kid – blue trousers of a material I don't recognise; a short-armed, collarless red shirt with a large white emblem on it; and black shoes with white markings. His hair is just a little shorter than mine, black and wavy. He has the same chin with a small dimple, the same nose (too small for his face) and the same angular cheeks. When he stops, even the way he stands is similar to me, with his hands down by his side, slightly to one side so his left eye is slightly further forward than his right.

To be honest, he could be a clone of mine. A weird clone, but definitely a clone. Yet, he doesn't seem like a clone. He is different in a way I can't explain.

We stare at each other for a few seconds, sizing each other up. He looks a little surprised as if he's working out why we look similar. I am aware, out of the corner of my eye, that the stars continue to fly past. They mustn't leave. I have made my decision.

I say it out loud. "Stay... stay!"

The strange boy speaks to me: "No! They must go!" Despite the echo which bounces his voice around, it's like listening to my voice. A desperate, angry version of my voice.

"You're wrong," I say after a pause. "They have to stay."

"They're evil. They have to go."

He's mad, but I'll try to talk reason into him. "No, they can't go – leaving will destroy them. I was angry with them, but now I want them to stay. If they leave, there will be nothing left. Surely you can see that?"

He seems desperate. "They tried to hurt me."

"They tried to hurt you because they don't want to be destroyed."

Self-defence! I'd do the same. Despite my Thor-like invincible impression earlier – convinced they should be destroyed – I am now convinced they should stay. There's nothing harmful in them. Rose-Anne said I would make the right choice. I can't let this idiot persuade me otherwise. I'm here to save the stars.

"They tried to hurt me," he repeats. "I'll make them pay for that."

He's acting like I was earlier. Power-hungry – another Thor!

"You're wrong," I tell him. "Leave them as they are."

He stiffens as if ready to act. I can feel the stars getting twitchy, like they're worried. This isn't going the way it should be going. Rose-Anne trusted me to do what's right and now I'm doing what's right, this old-fashioned dude is determined to mess it all up.

   It's time to show him who's in charge.

Marcus

The futuristic-looking boy does something I do not expect at all. He cries out. One word:

"Stay!"

One word that goes right through me, to my stomach where it bounces around for a while before working its way up and down and around my whole body, until all of me is vibrating with it. The boy takes a step towards me.

It is then that I realise the word has made a difference.

I look up, down, and then turn 360 degrees. The stars don't seem to be scared anymore. They are responding to the boy. Some rush past, do a complete circle, and fly past again and again. Others change direction and come past me from the top, the bottom or diagonally, only to appear again from a different direction. I sense that they are stronger for being together. They are ready to win this battle against me, and then return to their positions in the universe. I can feel it: they're ganging up, out to get me. And so, apparently, is this strange boy.

It's then that I suddenly start to feel very, very sick.

Shoal

Milo

The word "Stay!" bursts out of me and soon the stars are responding to me. Those that have begun their journey into nothingness, do an about-turn and come back, filing past in huge numbers. Proud, mighty and indestructible. I look across at my pairing. I am winning and he can do nothing against my force. The stars are with me. I am in control and I am sorry but this old copy of me is going to have to give in.

"I have made the right choice, Rose-Anne!" I shout. "I've saved the stars."

I'm not sure why but my pairing suddenly drops to the floor. He's on all fours, barely able to move. He lifts his head and looks at me. He looks dreadful: weak, his eyes are bloodshot and he's shaking. Sweat is dripping down his face and he is red; so, so red.

I make light work of the ten or so paces between us and, all of a sudden, I am over him, looking down on him. He lifts one hand towards me and mouths something that I can't understand before collapsing onto his stomach. I reach down and grab his shoulders, hauling him over onto his back. As I kneel next to him, I see that his eyelids are open, the brown pupils of his eyes huge, flicking from side to side. I see the reflection of my stars winking back at me. They are waiting now, happy in the knowledge they are safe. Safe to live on and on forever. I have saved them.

But what about the boy?

His breathing becomes shallower and I fear that, though I have stopped him from sending away the stars he might die because of it. He needs help. He lifts a hand, urging me to do something.

"Rose-Anne!" I call. "Rose-Anne, I've shown you that I care about the stars and I've done the right thing. But what about my pairing?"

He looks like he might die. This can't be right.

This can't be right at all!

Marcus

It's too much! The stars and the boy are too strong. I stutter and then fall to the floor. I try to crawl towards the boy. I want to fight, but I'm weak. I collapse, unable to move forward anymore.

Before I know it, I'm rolled over and, suddenly, the boy is above me. I stare up. And it's like looking into a mirror.

This is not the way it was supposed to be! All of that effort – travelling through the stars to get here. The ship, the conversations I had with Rose-Anne. She showing me how I could control the nightmares. Bringing Stefan back to help me. All of it wasted.

I don't feel at all well. I'm hot, far too hot. I can barely keep my eyes open.

Rose-Anne told me I had to make a decision: "At the right time, you will know what to do."

In that moment, I realise that I do know what to do. I was never here to protect the stars. I'm here to destroy them. They need to go. The problem is that I can't fight them. Not on my own.

I lift my hand. The boy stares at me, concern etched on his face. he calls out a name. "Rose-Anne."

Does he mean My Rose-Anne? How does he know her? I

want to ask him, but I'm too weak. I'm getting hotter by the second.

"Marcus?" I hear the boy say. "Marcus…"

But I'm slipping away.

All I want to do now is sleep… sleep… sleep.

Shoal

Milo

The boy closes his eyes.

"Marcus?" I say softly. "Marcus..." I call for Rose-Anne again, but there is no answer. No one answers. The stars have returned to their places in the sky, happy that I have done my job. Happy that I've saved them.

And it's about now, as I look down at my pairing, that I realise what Rose-Anne meant when she said I care. I look into his eyes and see the pain and suffering. He needs help. He's desperate for help.

"At the right time, you will know what to do," Rose-Anne had said.

Now is the right time. I look up, and the stars seem to laugh at me, him, both of us. Then it becomes obvious: the stars are doing this to him, the stars are making him sick.

After continually changing my mind, I do know what to do: I have to save Marcus. To do this, I have to destroy the stars. But am I too late? I look down. He's sick, so sick.

I raise my head, and scream out to the stars: "Go!"

Nothing happens. I shout it again: "Go!"

There's a moment when I think they have responded to me. They seem to freeze, and I look down at the boy again. His eyes had shut, but they flutter open momentarily. A sign, perhaps, that the stars are doing as I asked. A sign of hope.

But I'm wrong. Very wrong.

With the instinct of fish, once more they shoal. They come together into one massive, blindingly-bright, shoal. No swooping and sweeping past now. No movement at all – not even a quiver or a shimmer. They sit there above us; a mass of stars – together, sitting, waiting. Waiting to attack.

And then, suddenly, they dive and, like a swarm of bees, they're all over me… all over us. All that pain and sickness I felt a short while ago comes flooding back with a vengeance. I feel how the boy looks – weak, exhausted, desperate, like my head is going to explode.

The pain gets worse.

The sickness gets worse.

I collapse in a heap next to the boy, the tops of our heads nearly touching. powerless to stop the onslaught.

The stars are inside me now, streaming through my blood vessels. Like me when I travelled here, they're finding a way along the pathways to the centre. Towards my heart, my brain. On and on towards the very centre.

I can do no more.

I tried, Rose-Anne. I tried.

All I want to do now is sleep… sleep… sleep…

But then…

"Milo?... Milo?".

"Marcus?" I croak.

"We're ill," he says. "The stars are making us ill."

I see that now. Goodness knows, I feel it now. It's so painful, I can hardly think straight. I'm hot and getting hotter.

"Together," he says. "Let's do this together."

"How?" But I already know the answer. Rose-Anne had told me: *You will know.* She's right: I do know. "We fight."

"Yes,' he agrees, "we fight."

"Like Thor."

I hear a quiet chuckle. "Yes, like Thor."

"Together!"

"Together!"

And with that, we lock minds. I can feel us getting stronger… together. We grow stronger and stronger and we begin to fight back… together.

The stars inside us don't stand a chance. Our willpower is too much. Immediately, they start to leave our bodies.

When they shoal next, I know, and Marcus knows, that they will leave.

The stars are leaving.

And this time it will be for good.

Part 4 – To the End

Marcus

I want to open my eyes, but I can't. Every time I wake up and try to take a look around, I end up going straight back to sleep because it's far too much effort. My head feels like it's been removed from my shoulders and used as a basketball in a Bulls versus Knicks game.

Voices I don't recognise come and go. They are saying things that I can't make any sense of. More sleep and time passes until, after I don't know how long, I feel able to get those eyelids fully open.

When I do, things are blurry so I can't see things clearly, but what I can see tells me that I'm in hospital. There is a ceiling light directly above glaring at me, and to the lefthand side I can see a plastic bag with a tube coming out of it. I follow the tube down to my arm which is lying flat on top of folded white-starched sheets, the ones you get on every hospital bed. At the foot of the bed is a table with a jug of water and other bits and pieces I can't make out.

I want to look to the sides, but the ache in my head is

telling me that moving it isn't a good idea. I close my eyes again, figuring that I can use a bit of time to work out what I'm doing in a hospital again.

In hospital *again*? That's right; I remember that I spent time in one not that long ago after falling off a cliff. An accident that Stefan and I were both involved in it. We fell, but then what? I reach out for a memory, fail, and am about to give up when it all comes rushing back to me.

A journey on an incredible spaceship. The girl – Rose-Anne. Stefan was also there. A map to take me through the stars. I became ill. Very ill. Then the strange-looking boy – my pairing, Milo – looking down at me in concern. The stars attacking and we both became ill.

Not stars, perhaps? If not stars, something else then, but what?

Concerned, I start to drift away again, but then I become aware of sounds around me: the shuffling of feet, voices, children, the clink of a teaspoon. Ordinary sounds. My eyes flicker open.

A voice: "Did you see that? He opened his eyes! For a split second, I'm sure he did!"

It's the most wonderful voice in the world. I want to see the owner of that voice.

Mum.

"Marcus. you're awake! Oh, Marcus..." There's a hand on my hand, grasping it, stroking it. Another hand against my face. "Quickly, Sean, get a nurse or a doctor. Look, kids: your brother is awake!"

"Mum?"

A sob. "Yes, Marcus. It's me. We're all here. Your dad, Sean, Matilda, Joshua, Stefan. Stefan's been to see you every day."

I still can't move my head, but Mum's worried-looking face hovers into view and on the other side of it is Stefan, grinning like a Cheshire cat.

"Stefan?" I croak. "You got back ok?"

"Back? What are you talking about? I haven't been anywhere, apart from here. Good excuse to skip school."

"Skip school? It's the..." I can't think of the word I want to use to start with. "... the... the summer holidays, isn't it?"

"I wish!"

"Summer holidays finished a couple of months ago, love," Mum says.

"How are you, son?" It's Dad. My real dad. "You've had us very worried. We thought we'd lost you. You've been so ill for so long ..." His voice breaks and I hear sobs from others in the room.

Blimey! What on Earth has been going on?

I thought I had worked it all out – the spaceship, the stars, the battle at the end, and then they throw this bombshell onto me. I've been so ill for so long. What do they mean, ill? How did I get back here?

The arm without the tube in is picked up and my pulse is taken on the wrist. A thermometer is shoved into my mouth which stops me from asking any more questions, and a voice I don't recognise speaks.

"His pulse is fine, back to normal. Temperature..." – a plop sound as the thermometer is removed – "... is down, too. We will have to do more checks, but the fact he has come round is a good indication that Marcus is well on the way to making a recovery. Six months in a coma and he's suddenly come out of it. It's a miracle really."

There is laughter and words of relief, thanks given to the doctor. Sean is there and I get a "Welcome back, mate," from him and a pat on the back of the hand.

Mum – I hope it's Mum, anyway, and not Stefan – gives me a peck on the cheek. She is crying. I must have been bad for all of this reaction.

I want to join in the conversations that are going on all around me. It might help to fill in some of the gaps, but it's too much and I'm soon drifting off to sleep again.

When I wake up the next time, everyone's gone. Everyone except Rose-Anne who's right next to me.

"Marcus," she says. "Well done. You made the right choice in the end."

And then she explains what happened to me.

Shoal

Milo

I am in a medi-room with beeps and bongs going off in the background, shiny silver metal-plated walls all around and gentle, clean smells wafting through my nostrils.

My first thought is: who's the patient? And then, when I try to sit up and can't, I realise that the patient is me. There is a strap over my stomach which releases as soon as I move. I try to sit up again, but this time it's just the lack of energy in my body that stops me.

I don't feel great. I have a thumping pain at the back of my head and my eyeballs, unbelievably, ache. What am I doing here?

Rose-Anne's by my side. "You've been very unwell, Milo 8."

I can feel that. Tell me something I don't know!

"What happened to me?"

"You have just awoken from a coma."

"A coma?" This is serious stuff! "How long have I been in a coma?"

"Six of your Earth months."

Six months? "No way!"

"It is correct."

"I don't understand."

"You were unwell and now you are not. You have been on a sort of journey to help you get better."

"Yes! I remember. A journey through space."

"Not exactly through space, but to you it may have felt like a journey through space."

I hesitate and try and think that one through, but give up. Instead, I prompt her with another memory: "There was another me – or someone who looked like me. Weirdly-dressed dude."

"That's right. His name is Marcus. He is your pairing."

"Marcus... yes." I pause again: "Ah... I get it! That was another compulsoral." I study Rose-Anne's face for a moment. "You were in it... which means that this is a compulsoral too!"

Hah! I'm far too smart for them. They can't fool me.

"This is not a compulsoral. Nor was your experience with Marcus."

I don't believe her. I find myself beginning to describe what happened with the stars, the battle with the guy that looked like me. How he was ill. How I was ill. I do it to prove to her that I remember it all, and that I see it for what it is.

"I must admit," I say to her, "it was, and you are, a very realistic compulsoral."

"What you experienced, Milo 8, was, in its own way, very real."

I gabble on. "I beat the guy at the end. He wanted the

stars to leave, but I stopped him. And then I fell ill. We were both ill. And then we...."

What did we do? It doesn't matter, because it was a compulsoral and I...

She interrupts what I was about to say: "It was not a compulsoral. You and Marcus have truly been very ill."

"Look, there was no Marcus. It was a comp..." But I stop myself. Because she's looking at me very seriously.

"In the end – right at the end – you made the correct choice. Both of you did. The correct choice was not to save what you thought were stars. You worked together and defeated them."

I'm confused. "Weren't stars? What were they then?" I try to raise one eyebrow to look puzzled, like she does sometimes, but both go up. I must look like I've just seen a ghost.

Again, she gives me a serious look. "You have saved another's life, Milo 8."

"Whose life?"

"Marcus's life. As well as your own."

Then Rose-Anne explains who she is, where she's come from, and what the stars really were.

When she finally stops talking, I imagine both eyebrows are not only up, but they must spend the next ten minutes hovering way above my head.

Rose-Anne is a doctor. Apparently, I have been sick – so sick that I was in danger of being the latest of the Milo clones to depart from this world. That could not be allowed to happen for reasons that will become clear.

Rose-Anne and her alien pals have done some very clever mind-bending, medical stuff to cure me – or rather to help me cure myself. Those 'stars' that have been whirling about in my head for some years were not stars at all: they were a virus, germs that would eventually kill me. Although my body knew that it wanted to fight them and send them away, each time it tried, they just kept coming back. The virus evolved and kinda tricked me into wanting to save it – give into it – right up until the end.

None of the other Milos have had this problem; none of them, that is, except one. And he's not even called Milo. His name is Marcus and he was my pairing.

By joining forces, we fought off the virus, but we both had to make the right decision. We both had to realise what a danger those stars were, and our strength had to be combined to be rid of it. Mind-over-matter kind of stuff.

So, Rose-Anne helped us go on journeys through our minds, in our own special way, and get to the point where we could join up at exactly the same moment in time to send those stars – or germs – away into nothingness. None of what I experienced, from the time I first believed Rose-Anne was my girlfriend right up to me thinking I was Thor, travelling through the stars, was a compulsoral, nor did it actually happen. It was just me and my head.

Simple? Well... no.

That's where the time-travelling bit comes in. Because Rose-Anne is not any old doctor. She's a doctor from thousands of years in the future.

As for Marcus – he lived over three hundred years ago.

No compulsoral could come up with a storyline as whacky as this one.

Marcus

"Let me get this right," Stefan says as we lay flat our bikes on the grass next to the lake. "I'll try to repeat what you told me on the way up here."

We sit down and watch the sun glinting on the surface of the lake. There's a warm breeze and plenty of birdlife out taking advantage of the good weather. The atmosphere feels much lighter than when Stefan and I were here last time. Except, we didn't actually come up here at all, of course, something I've been trying to get straight in my mind and – even harder – explain in a logical way to Stefan.

I'm feeling much better, though I still get a little tired in the evenings. Stefan suggested this bike ride out to the lake to help get me moving more. Since most of it is uphill, I've had to take it real slow, but it has given us a chance to chat about all that has happened.

Stefan takes a glug from his water bottle, then starts to talk. "You say that I thought there was a spaceship which landed just over there." He points to the other side of the lake. "So, I persuaded you to come and have a look. We fell off the cliff and ended up in hospital. When we came back to check on the spaceship, you got taken away by an alien. So far, so good?"

"Yes."

"You flew through space in a ship like a bubble, felt sick, so turned it into the USS Enterprise. I joined you later, we went to your bedroom, got a map, and you used that to navigate from the edge of the universe to the centre. But it wasn't actually a map showing the way to the centre of the universe. It was like a map in your brain which helped you get to the source of the illness in your body." He gets up and takes a few paces towards the lake. "Except it didn't actually happen. Not that bit, anyway."

"It did and it didn't happen. I was guided on a journey in my head so I could get to the source of my illness. I know it sounds weird," I say to his back.

"To be honest," he says turning around and fixing his blue eyes on mine, "it sounds weird because it is weird. What you've described to me is a dream."

"It wasn't a dream."

"Things that happen inside your head are either dreams or thoughts. You do know that, don't you?"

"Yes! It was neither of those." I yank at a few blades of grass in frustration and toss them into the air. "I know it's hard to believe."

"That's not the only thing that's hard to believe, young Marcus."

I sigh. I'm not sure he's taking this very seriously now, although I'm quite impressed that he's replaying back so accurately what I've shared with him. At least it shows he was listening.

"So, let me be clear," he continues a little sarcastically. "In this journey which definitely wasn't a dream, you ended up at the centre of the universe, which was actually the centre of your body where all the illness came from, where you met this boy, your twin..."

"Pairing."

"What's the difference? If you're a twin, you're one of a pair."

"A twin is a brother or sister; Milo 8 is not my brother."

"Oh, yes – Milo 8. What a name! Okay, you met – actually met through some sort of mind connection – Milo 8. This is despite the fact that he lives – will live – three hundred years in the future?"

"Correct."

"And that bit's real; not a journey through your brain."

"It's real."

"Really real? Your brains, you say, connected... through time?"

"Yes."

"How?"

"I don't know exactly."

"Right. But your brains actually, in real life, connected through time?"

"Yes! You've just said exactly that."

"It's just that it's hard to take in."

"Well, take it in, because it's true."

"Marcus, connecting brains is impossible, even if you lived at the same time. When you're from different time periods…"

I'm getting cross now. Stefan can be annoying at the best of times. He's worse when he thinks he's right and I'm wrong. I jump to my feet. "Don't treat me like I'm stupid, Stefan!"

He puts his hands up. "Okay… Okay. I'll finish what I think you say happened next. It might help me understand better." He pauses. "Your twin…" I bunch my fists; he's winding me up on purpose. "… defeated you which meant the stars – which weren't stars – did not leave."

I nod. "But then he realised…"

"But then he realised his mistake right at the end and changed his mind. You then worked together to fight them off, and the stars left."

"Basically, yes. Working together gave us the strength to fight them off. If we hadn't joined forces, we both would have died."

"Of course. Oh, I nearly forgot to say… these stars move around in shoals, like fish. But they're not fish."

"They're not fish."

"Or stars."

"Or stars."

"They are – were, because you're cured now – a virus. Germs: the sort of thing you like looking at in your biology books." He starts pacing back and forth, head down in thought with his hands behind his back, acting like he's giving a lecture to students. "Each star or fish was a germ, part of the virus, which was inside attacking both of you, making you and your twin…"

I huff and roll my eyes. "Pairing."

"… making you and your twin pairing…"

My hands on hips and best glare are unlikely to stop him acting like this, but I give it a go because he's being deliberately awkward. "Just pairing."

"Right – making you and your pairing, very sick."

He stops pacing. Perhaps my glare worked. Maybe we can talk without him mucking about.

"Yes, the virus had been there since I was young," I explain. "Which is why I had nightmares about it. My body was telling me to reject the germs, send them away into nothingness, but I couldn't do it. They just turned into nightmares about the stars leaving."

Stefan gives me a look – part sympathy, part disbelief. Only Stefan can pull off a double-look like that. Somehow, he makes his next question sound just like his look. "Those nightmares happened, then?"

"Yeah. Don't you remember when I had really bad nightmares? Mum and Sean even took me to see a doctor."

"You saw a head doctor?"

"I know what you're thinking. Just because I saw a doctor back then, it doesn't mean I'm imagining this now. Something was wrong with my body, but I was too young to understand what it was, and not strong enough to fight it. The virus got worse recently and that's when I was taken to hospital and went into the coma. The doctors didn't know what was wrong with me, if you remember, then I suddenly got better. They don't know how, but I did. That proves I had some outside help."

"Hmmm."

"Stefan: you know how close I was to dying."

His face clouds over. "I do. It was horrible to watch. And I couldn't do anything."

"No, you also helped me. You were part of the journey I was on while I was in the coma. I'm not sure I would have got through without you."

He smiles, slightly embarrassed. Stefan and I don't do soppy stuff. But I felt he needed to know how important a part he played.

He coughs, perhaps keen to move the subject on. "So, your future-self went on a journey while he was in a coma too? If he hadn't, he would've died."

"Yes, except his journey and experiences were different, more based on his life. You've still not got this: he's not my future-self. He's a clone of me who lives in the future."

"As in a clone that does circus tricks?" In an instant, we're back to the much less serious, disbelieving Stefan.

"Very funny. There's only one clown round here, and that's you."

"I'm still confused. He came back through time to save you?"

"No, no. I told you: it didn't work like that."

"How did it work, then, and how come you've got a clone? One of you is bad enough, but a dozen running around spilling crisps on the floor, burping all the time and not sharing your Pokémon cards, just doesn't bear thinking about."

"Rose-Anne explained it like this..."

He jumps in before I can go on: "So, she is real?"

I pick up a pebble and skim it across the lake. Pleasingly, it bounces at least nine times. That will wind Stefan up. His record is only seven.

"She's real. She visited me in hospital. Showed me how to go on this journey through my mind and body."

"And she's a doctor, you say?"

"Yes, a proper medical doctor, from thousands of years in the future. That bit's more complicated."

"Sounds very unlikely, but I'm prepared to hear you out, Marcus. I've got time; I'm not going anywhere until I've beaten that ridiculous skimming record you've produced!"

Milo

I've moved on from doing the freighter pilot work. It's a relief. It was basically the same thing every single day – a different spot on the planet, but the same routine. Now I'm doing something much better! I've been fast-tracked onto the Interstellar Cadet programme.

Ahead of me is six months of flight training (which basically involves playing computer games all day – yes!) and then I'll be transferred to the new space station, right on the very edges of the solar system. From there, I'm hoping I will be launched into a glittering new career as a space explorer.

I've been told that they are about to bring out a new spaceship – the MRX3.4. It's lightning fast (getting much closer to the speed of light, they reckon), sleeker and much more sensible than the ones they have at the moment which take years to get to our nearest star. I'd be an old man – at least twenty-one – before I got to the closest star, Alpha Centauri, in the old tin cans they use at the moment!

So, life is good. I have a bigger box to live in. I enjoy my training, I'm being noticed because of my new Space Explorer uniform, and I can buy whatever I like whenever I like, without being told what I should be buying.

That's a real bonus of the new job, not having to do the

compulsorals anymore. I can choose to if I want to, but so far, I've not wanted to. Why would I? They're nowhere near as exciting as being visited by a doctor of the future and taken on a mad ride through my brain to get cured.

I have a lot more credits to spend too, and I use a couple now to order my favourite drink, a Fizzbanger – orange, pineapple, lemonade, and sherbet to give it that kick, served with popping sparklers sticking out the top. Within seconds, there's a swishing sound in the chute and the light's on to say it's arrived. Just what I need to keep me hydrated while I do an extra bit of study. (In other words, play another game!)

I take a couple of slurps and then switch on my Stella Study Pack. Immediately, my box is transformed into the virtual world of the flight deck on the MRX3.4. This time, I'm hoping they will teach me how to stop this mean machine! It's all very well travelling at close to the speed of light, but if you can't slow the thing down to take a look at the stars, there's no point going in the first place.

I get myself comfortable in my mega-comfy seat (it's so cool – I use it all the time, even when I'm not training) and prepare myself to pick up where I left off last time.

Life is good. I have a bright future, and so does the human race, thanks to me and Marcus.

Why is everyone's future so bright? Well, Rose-Anne has told me exactly what I will become. I'm going to be the

Interstellar Cadet who becomes the Interstellar Pilot in charge of the first spaceship to travel at the speed of light. Because of that, breakthroughs in time travel will happen that end up producing people – including alien people, because humans will be able to go far enough to meet them – that can travel through time and help fix the mess the human race is in at the moment. People like Rose-Anne.

If Marcus and I hadn't saved each other, none of that will ever happen.

It'll take patience and time, Rose-Anne has explained, but thanks to her – and Marcus – I have that time now. Time to grow up properly. Time to care. Time to think about things and make the right choices. Time I wouldn't have had if Marcus and I hadn't got rid of those germs.

Germs that looked like stars that looked like shoaling fish.

Marcus

"You are starting to freak me out now, Marcus," says Stefan.

He's still confused but he's also in a huff, mainly because he's tried – and failed miserably – to beat my skimming record while we have been talking.

"So, you know already," he goes on, "that when you grow up, you will be the scientist that designs, makes and becomes the first human clone. Isn't that a bit weird?"

"What, already knowing that I will be that scientist, or making a clone of myself?"

"Both."

"They are connected. Because I know I will be the first person to make the first clone of themselves, it kinda helps me want to do it even more."

"And – to be clear – this Milo 8 is one of your clones?"

"Yes. I make a clone that becomes another clone and so on until, eventually, Milo 8 is made. And because Milo 8 will become the first pilot to travel at the speed of light, he sets the path for discovering that when you go at those speeds, you can go back in time. By the time Rose-Anne is around, thousands of years in the future, they have discovered all sorts of things, including both how to travel back in time and how to use the power of our brains over different time periods to cure diseases."

"And they used Milo 8, rather than another clone because he had the same sickness as you?"

"Yep. We were a good fit, I guess. Same genes and same illness, which meant we could fight the illness together."

"I'm finding this difficult to take in."

He throws a stone high up into the air and it lands in the lake with a loud plop about five metres away. He then turns around and fixes his eyes onto me with an expression that tells me he is in no way convinced.

I hold his gaze for a few seconds and then say, "You think I've made all of this up?"

"Well, it does sound a bit unlikely, doesn't it? I know you love biology and want to do great things, but being the scientist who makes the biggest breakthrough ever in human cloning. Really? Then there's all this time travel nonsense. Come on! Perhaps all that time in the coma has made your brain go..." He hesitates, perhaps searching for words that I won't find insulting. He doesn't find them. "...made your brain go loopy."

"You think I've gone mad?"

"No... I mean, yes... Oh, I don't know. Maybe, Marcus."

"I need you to believe me, Stefan. You're my best friend. If you don't believe this happened, I may not believe it all myself, and do what I need to do in the future."

I feel exhausted. The weeks since I left the hospital have

been a slog. I've been itching to share my story. Now I have done it, my best mate thinks I've made it all up.

"Perhaps you shouldn't believe it either, Marcus," he says. "You were very ill, remember? This all sounds like one big dream. I'm sorry, I'm being honest and telling you that for your own good."

Suddenly, I have doubts. As sure as I was, the whole thing could have been one long dream. Six months asleep is certainly plenty enough for my brain to convince me that Rose-Anne was real and not out of my imagination.

Time travel... clones... what was I thinking?

"Maybe..." I say, "maybe, you're right."

Maybe it's easier to forget the whole thing. Maybe it's best to just act normally and forget Rose-Anne, fish, stars, germs, and fighting off illness with a boy from the future. Most of that was in my head anyway; perhaps it all was.

"Here, try this one," I say, throwing Stefan a perfect flat pebble I had been rubbing in my hand. He catches it and nods his thanks. I watch him take his shoes and socks off and wade a few paces into the lake. He is making a big show of trying to beat my record.

"Watch and learn," he grins. "Watch and learn." He lifts up one leg and leans back, ready to throw, then suddenly stops, frozen to the spot.

He's seen something near the bushes that I haven't.

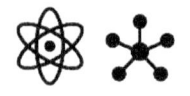

Marcus and Milo

"I wish I could meet Marcus, Rose-Anne. You know, properly, face to face, not just through our minds. He sounds an intelligent guy... like me."

"Yes, he is like you, Milo 8. Very much like you."

"Can I? Can I meet him? You've travelled through time. You're with me now, which proves you know how to do it."

"It is possible but would be highly unusual. Yet..." She stops for a moment and listens as if she is checking something. "Yet, it seems it is necessary."

"Huh? Necessary?"

"Yes, it seems it is necessary. There is hesitation from your pairing, Marcus. He has doubts which means he may not go on to do what he must do. An adjustment is necessary so that the timelines are complete."

I don't know what she means by adjustment to the timelines, but I'm pleased, so I say, "That's fantas..."

And then I'm standing by a bush, next to a lake. And this boy I don't recognise is standing in a strange position, his left leg up and his right arm pulled back as if he is about to throw something. He looks a little bit uncomfortable... and somewhat surprised to see me.

I can't help but smile, and then I roar with laughter as he stares at me before overbalancing and falling sideways into the shallows of the water.

A familiar laugh joins in, and then I see an equally familiar face walking towards me.

"Hello, Milo 8," the face says.

"Hello, Marcus," I say. "Good to see you again. Been fishing recently?"

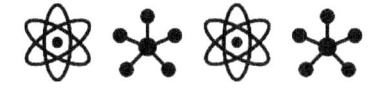

Shoal

Acknowledgements

I was lucky to be a teacher. You can learn a lot from children, and they, indirectly and directly, helped me to write this book.

How so indirectly? Well, teaching children to write made me ensure the skeleton onto which I fleshed out the story was solid. It's hard to forget full stops and how to put together an adverbial phrase when you've been drumming those things into children for over 15 years. Also, children love stories. I wanted them to love Shoal. It helped to keep me focussed and my imagination soaring.

How so directly? I did author visits after I had just begun this book and gave excerpts to children so they could give me feedback. I read every piece of feedback and, like a good learner, I took it on board.

Though I can't mention all the children by name, I said I would give a shoutout to the schools I went into. So, thank you to all those children and to the following schools for having me:

Montgomery Junior School, Colchester

North Primary, Colchester

Birch C of E Primary

Ingatestone & Fryerning Primary

Tiptree Heath Primary

St Teresa's Primary, Colchester

St Thomas More Primary, Colchester

St Mary's Senior School, Colchester

St Albans Catholic High School, Ipswich.

Special thanks to Michele-Christine Luthra, Kayleigh McDonald, and Asiya Siddiqi from North Primary for reading advanced copies and giving feedback.

A special mention to the staff and children at Gosbecks Primary and North Primary in Colchester, where I spent most of my teaching career.

About the Author

For many years, Ian was a primary school teacher in his home town of Colchester in the UK. Then he went on holiday to New Zealand, and everything changed. Standing by a stunning lake in Glenorchy in the South Island, he had an idea for a book. There and then, he decided to give up his teaching job so that he could do what he had always wanted to: write a novel.

That book was Quarton: The Bridge, the first in the Quarton science fiction trilogy, written for young adults. Since then, he has written books for adults, a play, and well over one-hundred 100-word stories for radio. He also writes blogs and, being retired now, occasionally pops into school to remind himself what fun it is to teach children.

SHOAL is his first book for children. Later this year, he plans to release his second children's book about a time-travelling girl from the future who travels back in time to fix things that have gone wrong.

Contacts

Ian would love to know what you think of his books, so why not leave a review on Amazon or Goodreads?

Or contact Ian on the social media links below:

Website www.ianhornett.com

Facebook @ianmichaelhornett

Instagram @ianhornett

Other books by Ian Hornett

'The Quarton Trilogy' for young adults

Quarton: The Bridge

Quarton: The Coding

Quarton: The Payback

All books available on Amazon in paperback and as an e-book.

See the next page for the blurb to the first in the series – Quarton: The Bridge.

Quarton: The Bridge

Surviving in a city devastated by a nuclear attack, Fen has had to be resourceful, resilient and ready for anything. The discovery of the quarton block – the one remaining stone created to power a bridge between two worlds – lures her in and throws her already dangerous life as a scavenger into turmoil.

Fen suddenly finds herself traveling a path that was set for her in a previous life on an alien planet, thousands of years ago.

But there are others who have been pulled into the quarton's domain. Like Fen, they have lived many times before. And they exist for one purpose: to claim the last quarton.

What started as a battle for personal survival has become a battle to decide the future of two worlds.

Shoal

Printed in Great Britain
by Amazon